LONG SHOT

BY

MARIE FOWLER

www.scobre.com

Scobre Press Corporation
2255 Calle Clara
La Jolla, CA 92307

Scobre Press books may be purchased for educa-
tional, business or sales promotional use.

First Scobre edition published 2003.

Edited by Debra Ginsberg
Copyedited by Gina Zondorak
Illustrated by Larry Salk
Cover Design by Michael Lynch

ISBN 0-9708992-6-2

TOUCHDOWN EDITION

www.scobre.com

CHAPTER ONE

THE LIST

"Put it up!" I screamed, as Clarissa drove past both defenders. She released a hook shot over the top of Tree Hastings, our close friend and the biggest guy on campus. Her rainbow arched high above his outstretched arms and passed through the orange rim. Swish! The sweet sound of nothing but net.

Pick-up games——that's what Clarissa and I were reduced to after our final college season. Of course, these weren't just ordinary pick-up games. We managed to get a few guys we were friends with to play two-on-two against us. The guys were a few shades shy of great, but what they lacked in talent they made up for with size.

"Shoot!" Clarissa and I bellowed, trying to rattle Rob Coker, who was standing at the top of the key. He always dribbled between his legs for no reason and was constantly

smiling at us. I slapped the ball away from him, "Get real, Rob." Not only did he think he had a chance at beating us, but he would ask me out after almost every game.

I put up a short jumper that kissed off the glass and dropped through the hoop. "Twenty-six, all!" I called out.

Rob was still talking trash, "Is that all you've got, Brit?" He dribbled right toward me shifting left at the last minute, expecting to leave me flatfooted in his wake. But I anticipated him and snatched the ball.

When I got back to the three-point line I stopped. Rob's momentum had him jumping past me, and I calmly flipped one toward the basket, nothing but net.

"That's three, Robbie."

"That's luck, Brit."

"That's game, guys," Clarissa laughed. "Good thing too, 'cause I'm getting pretty hungry."

When we played against the guys, the prize was always dinner. "I think I feel like burgers tonight," I taunted Rob and Tree from the top of the three-point line, shooting one more swish and looking over at Rob. "I guess that was luck, too." I knew how to handle these guys. I'd grown up with an older brother and played plenty of basketball against the boys.

It was early April, March Madness was long forgotten, and the World University Games in Mexico City still a pleasant memory. I moved like a zombie. Today was the day that I would find out about the Olympic trials and I'd been nervous since I awoke that morning.

After four years as a point guard for the Shooting Stars, I was getting ready to leave the University of Northern Vir-

ginia. What was next——I had no idea. Although my teammates all seemed to have their engines revving for the future, I was stuck in neutral. Ming was slated to begin graduate school at Long Island State and Andrea was getting married to Cliff Lang, her high school sweetheart. Clarissa was headed to the WNBA and the Milwaukee Score, while most of the other girls had another year or two left of school.

I was a twenty-two-year-old, five-foot-six-inch point guard who hadn't been drafted. My jumper from the top of the key was great, you could take it to the bank, but it wasn't enough to impress pro scouts. Still, I had hope. I was going to try out for a WNBA team even if they didn't have the foresight to draft me.

I packed up my stuff and left the gym, heading back to the dorms to pick up my camera for a class later that day. Clarissa stuck around the gym to try and convince Coach Hollins to let her in on who'd been invited to Olympic tryouts.

I walked out into the mild April air. A soft breeze was blowing. The yellow daffodils and purple crocus were springing up underfoot, making the air smell sweet. The dogwood trees were budding and robins were singing. I breathed in deep. I love spring, I thought. Actually, I could never decide if it was spring or fall that was my favorite. Summer definitely was not. I spent most of my summers working or training at one basketball camp or another. I still get tired just thinking about all the laps I ran in the August heat. As for winter, well, winter was game time. Or used to be, anyway. I wondered what I would be doing during the rest of the winters of my life. I hoped I'd be playing basketball somewhere.

While on campus, I bounced a ball everywhere I went. The more I dribbled, the better my handle was. As a point guard, your ability to dribble the ball is everything. You have to be in total control or your entire team will crumble. You're the leader on the floor, the eyes, ears, and heart of your team. This was what I loved about playing point guard: the choices I made on every play dictated the game. If I wanted to run, we ran. If I slowed it down, we'd dig in our heels and bang inside. I was the captain, the lead singer, the quarterback, the pilot, the pitcher, the——

"Brittany, wait up!" A voice came from behind me, breaking my thought.

I slowed my dribble and saw Clarissa racing up the walk to catch me. "I got the word on tryouts," she shouted with a new burst of adrenaline. "Los Angeles! Middle of June!" My heart was in my throat. Knowing where the tryouts were to be held was only half the battle. In order to try out for the United States Olympic team, a player had to be specifically asked to attend the trials. Though I was sure Clarissa would be invited, I doubted that I would. I wasn't even drafted by a pro team, so being chosen to represent my country was a long shot.

"Come on," Clarissa beamed, tugging at my arm. "Coach has the list."

We raced back to the gym, heading for the locker room and the invite list. Coach Hollins was standing in her office holding the paper above her head as a group of us begged her for a peek. Clarissa, six-feet-three-inches tall and very strong, had no trouble jerking the list from Coach's hands and scan-

ning it quickly. She was always one to confront things head on. Me, I wanted it so badly that I was afraid to look.

"We're in," Clarissa shouted, giving me a hug.

"We?" I said, looking at her like she was crazy.

"We're going to LA!" she yelled, shaking her head so that the bright purple beads braided into her dark hair clattered and sparkled under the hot fluorescent lights. I clumsily dropped the basketball and it fell right on my toe. Clarissa read, "Los Angeles, California, June 15, to try out for," she paused for emphasis, and ended up screaming, "the United States Olympic Basketball Team!"

I couldn't believe my ears and I snatched the list away to see for myself. Sure enough, there I was—Brittany Bristol, Northern Virginia.

"Who else made it?" Clarissa asked, looking over my shoulder. "Starling!" she gasped in mock surprise. I nodded. Sherry Sterling, my biggest rival since high school, would be trying out for the same guard position as I would. Clarissa was my closest friend, but even she couldn't resist a cackle of amusement. "Better watch the room assignments, Brit, old Starling'll be after you."

We called Sherry Sterling "Starling" because the UNV campus had been plagued by a flock of the pesky, pitch-black birds the fall of our junior year. Everything the groundskeepers did to discourage them would entice more of them to come. They were everywhere. Finally, the birds got to be a big joke. The student council showed that old Alfred Hitchcock movie The Birds, getting a bunch of guys to dress up in some borrowed mascot costumes. It was actually really funny, and the starlings got blamed for everything bad that happened on campus.

So when Sherry showed up on the court and they called out her name "Sherry Sterling," the name Starling was just a natural. It helped that she had long, dark hair, too. I suppose you could say she was pretty but I disliked her, so it would have been hard for me to admit it. On the court, Sherry would stoop to any dirty trick in the book. There was no reason for it either because she was a really good player. She had the best three-point shot in women's college basketball. But still, Sherry played her games. Like faking an injury the minute the momentum swung against her team, or tripping a player as she drove toward the basket. That kind of thing got to all of us, but most of all to me. It was probably because I'd known her the longest. I had to put up with Sherry in high school when she played for our big cross-town rival, Shenandoah.

And then there was the matter of Brian, my brother Eric's best friend. I adored Brian from the time I could do nothing but tag along after him. By junior year, he was the great love of my life—not that he knew this, mind you. I was nothing more than Eric's kid sister to him.

I was brought back from my daydreaming again by Clarissa, "Time to celebrate, Brit."

I left Starling and Brian in the back of my head and sat down at a long wooden table in Everett Hall, the cafeteria I'd been eating in for the past four years. Clarissa and I were going to be trying out for a spot on the Olympic team and at least fifteen others joined in the celebration. The University of Northern Virginia is a small school about twenty-five miles outside *of Washington, D.C., not too far from Oak Grove, Virginia, where I grew up. I looked at a lot of schools before I decided on UNV, but it all came down to a great art program, a basketball team that I hoped needed my help, and the not-too-shabby academic scholarship they offered me. I've never been sorry. I've had a lot of great times, some trying times, and I've grown up a lot here. That happens no matter what, I suppose, but UNV was the place where it happened to me.*

We ordered The Special: twelve scoops of different kinds of ice cream smothered in hot fudge. With the trials coming up in less than two months, we'd have to take our training to a new level. This was our last big splurge and we decided to make it a good one. Jen and Andrea hovered over our shoulders on one side, and Tree reached over the top of everyone's head to swipe large dollops of chunky cherry. Rob nudged in so close he nearly knocked me off my stool.

I spaced out while everyone around me talked and ate. I began to focus on the particulars. The trials would be held at Los Angeles State. The thought of traveling cross-country to Los Angeles was exciting in itself. As far as I could tell, the biggest downside was the group of coaches making selections. There were three. One I knew only by reputation and one coached a team we played often. What really gave me butterflies was the third member of the selection team. She was the head coach of Northern California State, the team that had beaten us in the final game of my college career. She was a terrific strategist and motivator, having devised a plan that held our team to its lowest point total of the season. But (and this was a big but), there was the matter of the three players on her own team invited to the trials. She had to feel some allegiance to "her" girls. How could I possibly have a chance?

"Wake up, Brit!" Clarissa hit me on the wrist with her spoon. "Strawberry's about gone."

I dug back into The Special quickly. Strawberry ice cream was my favorite, just as Clarissa's was vanilla. And like good buddies, we looked out for one another. Looking back, it's pretty amazing that we ended up best friends, because we certainly didn't start out that way at UNV. I came in, hoping to be on the team. Clarissa came in, expecting to be the star. Or at least that's what we all thought. It took her a long time to warm up to people when she first came here.

We've always been very different, especially on the basketball court. Clarissa is tall. She plays center and probably has the best hook shot of any player on earth, college or pro, male or female. That hook brought us a lot of success over the past couple of years. I'm a little point guard, a playmaker, more than a pure shooter. I don't have the size to play forward and I don't have much speed or a wide variety of shots, either. In fact, people who don't know me are always amazed when they find out I'm a basketball player.

My one great beauty is my long reddish-blonde hair. It took me a while to grow it out just perfectly, but I finally got it right during my junior year. I don't mean to suggest that I'm a cover girl, but guys are surprised to learn that I'm an athlete. (Why do they always think cute girls can't play sports?)

Basketball-wise, what I really have going for me is what Coach says, I "keep my head in the game." And hey, I'm a good foul shooter, an underappreciated skill not to be dismissed.

I've held the school record, the conference record, and believe it or not, this year, I had the NCAA record.

Of course, my brother Eric claims he and Brian ought to get the credit, because of all the years they let me practice with them. If I missed a foul shot, they wouldn't let me touch the ball for the next five minutes. They took turns driving at the basket and I had to try and stop them. In the beginning, I think it was their way of trying to get rid of me. But I was too stubborn for that. In the end, I learned how to shoot from the free-throw line and I got pretty good at defending.

"Split the mint chip with me," Clarissa broke into my thoughts again. "We'll be back to training after this."

"Does that mean we can't even treat ourselves after exams?" I asked.

Clarissa shook her head firmly. "And not after graduation, either."

I moaned, beginning to think that maybe we weren't so lucky after all.

Jen, our junior forward, banged her spoon on the table. "Get with the program, Brit. The rest of us are counting on y'all. This is the Olympics."

"Yeah," agreed Leesha, "you make the team, we'll treat you to all the ice cream you can eat."

"I'd sell my soul for a chance like this." Jen added, sneaking a bite of vanilla when Clarissa wasn't looking.

"You told me last week that you'd sell your soul for a date with Jack Redman." Clarissa laughed. "Your soul's cheap, girl."

I glanced at my watch and wiped away my smile. "I've

got to run. Photography class." I stood and Leesha thrust a basketball at me. "Don't waste time, Brit, dribble everywhere."

I hesitated, but Clarissa piped up quickly, "You know Starling's dribbling somewhere right now." How could I argue with them? She probably was. I took the ball and dutifully bounced my way across campus toward Patriot Hall, the fine arts building. During my four years at UNV, I probably spent as much time there as I did in Hamilton Gym. I came here as a freshman, and soon decided I'd be a great painter like Georgia O'Keeffe. Fascinated with those big, glorious flowers that filled her canvases, I spent hours copying her works and drew hundreds of flowers myself.

After a month or so, my drawing teacher recommended working from photographs since most of my early drawings lacked something. OK, they stunk. Anyway, I thought this was a pretty good idea since I had a photography requirement to fulfill anyway. Between the UNV campus and a couple of historic houses in the area that had extensive gardens, I found a lot of flowers to photograph. In the end, I discovered it was photography, and not flowers or painting that I really loved. It's funny how life happens that way sometimes. Just when you think you've figured out what you want, you find out what you really want by accident. Look at all those hours I spent as a kid, playing basketball with Eric and Brian, just to be included, just to make them notice me. Who would have guessed I'd end up liking it so much?

I walked through the "quad," a big concrete square with a fountain in the center. We'd always toss in change when we passed to make a wish. I smiled, remembering when

Clarissa, Ming, Jen, and I celebrated the end of winter exams by putting detergent in the fountain. Bubbles everywhere for days. When I reached the fountain I searched my pockets for coins. The only coin I had was my lucky Washington State quarter. There was no way I could throw that one away. It had been bringing me good luck since high school. Oh well, what more could I wish for today anyway?

I took the shortcut to Patriot Hall, veering around the library and past Wilson North, my freshman dorm. There was an open window on the second floor and I heard music coming from inside. Oh no, not the piano, I thought, kicking a rock. I stopped bouncing the ball and hurried down the stone walk. I couldn't get out of there fast enough. If there's one thing I had enough of when I was a kid, it was the piano.

CHAPTER TWO

A NATURAL

I finally hit the wall with piano lessons right around my fourteenth birthday. And yes, I will admit that the lessons were my idea in the first place. Lots of my friends were learning when I was about eight, and I thought it looked like fun. So I pestered Mom and Dad until they gave in. My grandmother had a piano she wasn't using anymore, so Dad borrowed a truck and they moved it into our family room. It was a really big ordeal.

Eric said that he didn't want any part of piano lessons, but I was pretty sure he was jealous. I really liked playing in the beginning and the recitals weren't too bad because I always got to pick out a new dress. Of course, this also meant that I had to learn a new song by heart. And I didn't mind that much at first. The problem was, every year the music got harder and harder to memorize.

By the fall of my freshman year of high school, I decided I'd rather spend Monday afternoons doing something else. I fell out of love with the piano as life got more complicated. After all, I was fourteen years old! I wanted to hang out with my friends and go to the mall or the movies. But Mom wasn't having it. She reminded me that when we got Gran's piano, I promised to take lessons all the way through high school. I couldn't believe that I made that deal. What was I thinking?

"Brittany!" Mom yelled up the stairs and I knew what she wanted. I sighed, realizing there was no getting out of it. It was Monday afternoon and I was supposed to have gone directly to Mrs. Ripley's house after school. Instead, I crept up the stairs into my bedroom to check my e-mail. "Brittany, come downstairs right now." Mom sounded a little angry this time. I quickly shut off the computer and bolted down the stairs. By the time I reached the bottom step, Mom was out front honking the horn. I climbed in the car, knowing I was in for a lecture on the way to Mrs. Ripley's.

"You forgot again, Brittany," Mom scolded.

"Sorry," I tried to sound sincere, but, honestly, I would just as soon have skipped the whole thing.

"Remember what we said when you started with the piano, Brittany."

"I know, I know," I nodded, "Always finish what you start." We pulled into Mrs. Ripley's driveway and I asked Mom one last time, "But can I please quit this one time?"

Her answer was a definitive "No."

After lessons, I didn't take the quickest route home. It was still nice out and the late October sky was bright blue and crystal clear. Virginia was just about the prettiest place on earth this time of year. A squirrel scurried across the sidewalk in front of me as I walked down Magnolia Lane. I heard the bouncing of a basketball, followed by taunting and scuffling. Eric and his best friend Brian were playing one-on-one. Although I'd never admit it to them, their game was the reason I took this "shortcut" to begin with. I knew they'd be outside shooting hoops, they always were.

Brian's dog, a brown and white terrier named Max, bounded over to greet me as I made my way to the foot of the driveway. Naturally, the boys didn't see me——or pretended they didn't, anyway. "Good boy," I said, scratching him behind his furry white ears. He dropped a shoe at my feet and started to play tug of war with it. "Sorry, Max, I bet that belongs to Brian, you're not getting me into trouble." I tossed it over on the porch and turned my attention back to the game. It didn't take long before an errant pass came my way. I snagged it and dribbled a few times.

"Come on, Brit, give it back," Eric shouted.

I ignored my brother, grinning at him while I dribbled. Brian charged at me a moment later, knocking me to the ground playfully and grabbing the ball. He helped me up and I raced after him, Max at my heels. "Please, guys, let me play," I moaned.

"Get lost," Eric ordered, refusing to glance in my direction.

Brian's eyes met mine. He took the ball over to the end of the driveway and shouted to Eric, "OK, you make it from here or your sister plays."

I smiled at Brian.

Eric scowled, knowing a shot from the end of the driveway was nearly impossible to make. He let it fly anyway and when it bounced off the top of the backboard I raced forward and caught it. "Fine, two-on-one," Eric shouted. My heart sunk for a moment. It didn't take a genius to figure out who the "one" would be. I didn't care though, I was playing and that's all I wanted.

Stealing the ball would be my best chance at a shot, so I kept my hands loose and ready. It didn't take more than a couple of drives toward the basket before I was able to slap one away from Eric. I dribbled back up the driveway, keeping my body between Brian and the ball. "Not bad, Brit," he spoke and swatted at the same time, "You should try out for the girls' team."

I was so surprised by this comment that I almost picked up my dribble. Did Brian mean that or was he just trying to distract me? The girls' team. I'd never really given that any thought. I gazed at Brian. Just looking at his blue eyes made my heart skip a beat. Eric was there quickly to ruin my moment, "Yeah, like she has a chance." He tried to grab the ball from me.

I stepped to the side of them both and took a poorly aimed shot. It bounced past the garage and into a rose bush, sending Max scurrying for cover.

Brian retrieved it, "You've got to work on that shot, though." He spoke softly as he passed me and then shouted, "Let's play horse, Eric."

"Not again," Eric groaned.

Brian insisted, "We have to help your sister out, she needs a lot of work on her jump shots if she expects to make the team." Brian was trying to include me and for a moment I wondered why. I looked at him and just as his blue eyes met mine Eric shouted,

"Well stop staring at one another and let's play."

Brian blushed, embarrassed, "I wasn't staring at her." He threw up a shot, "Shut up and let's play, Eric."

I tried to smile over at Brian, but he didn't really look at me for the rest of the game. Still, I was starting to feel pretty excited about the idea of trying out for the girls' team.

We shot hoops until Brian's mom called him in for supper about an hour later. Then Eric and I walked the two blocks to our house, taking turns dribbling. He always treated me better when I was the only one around. "So how's freshman year going?" he inquired, bouncing the ball off the wrought iron fence around Smith Clove Park.

"So far, so good," I answered. "Math's OK, English, too. But I really like physics."

Eric made a face. "That's only because you're good at drawing stuff. I couldn't wait to get out of there."

A car passed and the horn honked. Eric waved.

"Who's that?" I asked, curiously. I knew he'd never volunteer the information.

"Susan Ambler," he mumbled.

"The cheerleader?"

"Yeah."

I rolled my eyes. "Don't tell me you're interested in her? She's got to be the most stuck-up person in the whole school." None of the girls at Jefferson High could bear Susan Ambler. She probably didn't have a single girlfriend. Then again, I suppose she didn't need us, the boys were tripping over each other for her. It was sickening. And to think that my brother was falling for her was just too much.

"Hey," Eric scolded, "She's cool. Besides, it's Brian she likes."

"Don't tell me that Brian—" I stopped myself, more annoyed now than I'd been when I thought Eric was the object of her attention.

He nodded. "He talks to her all the time."

I kicked at a rock in frustration. Eric broke the silence. "Why do you care?"

"I don't. I was just—"

Eric cut me off, "Race you home." He took off, knowing he'd caught me off guard. I gave chase, but he still beat me out by a hair.

Tryouts for the junior varsity girls' team took place in the middle of October. Junior varsity, or JV, was a high school team comprised of freshman and sophomores. This was the team you played on before varsity. I was extra nervous because I hadn't played any school sports before and I didn't really know what to expect. Despite the fact that Eric and Brian drove me crazy working on free throws since I was twelve, I was sure I couldn't possibly make the team. There were about forty girls trying out for just fifteen spots.

On the day of tryouts, I wore my lucky tee shirt from Virginia Beach and laced up my brand new high tops. I hadn't planned on wearing them, but Brian said I was crazy not to break them in. Jefferson had a new basketball coaching staff this year. The guy in charge of the JV team was Coach Buzz Holt. He was a Jefferson graduate who'd gone on to play at Duane University. He was really tall and spoke in the deepest voice I'd ever heard.

As soon as I entered the gym, Coach threw a bunch of basketballs onto the court and told us all to warm up for about ten minutes. Warm up? I hadn't even changed yet. The sophomores immediately took over, pretty much playing keep-away. Some of the more courageous freshmen tried to steal a ball here and there, but we were no match for the experience or the attitude of the older girls.

In no time, Coach Holt had divided us up into four squads to run drills. We spent about an hour dribbling up and down the court, passing the ball back and forth, and forming lines for layup drills, right handed, then left. When we finished those drills Coach took out a role of black electrical tape and made marks all over the court. We were to dribble to each mark and fire a shot at the basket without hesitation. This was something I'd never practiced. I soon figured out that shooting off the dribble is much more difficult than a set jumper.

Coach watched this drill carefully. I dribbled the ball off my toe once and made a little less than half my shots. I'd say my performance was about in the middle of pack. We then went over to shoot free throws, where I always looked good. I was glad this was the last thing Coach Holt saw of me before sitting us down in the bleachers.

"Y'all are real good, so give yourselves a round of applause." He began his speech with a broad smile and a thick Southern accent. Everyone applauded but the tension in the air remained thick. I sat in the top row of the bleachers, fidgeting uncontrollably, unable to coax my hands into clapping. "Anyway, I'd like to take another look at some of you before I make my selections. So if I call your name, I'd like you to come back here tomorrow and we'll go through the drills again." He paused a moment. "If I don't call your name, thank you for coming out. Keep practicing and try again next year."

Suddenly I wished I hadn't worn a bright orange tee shirt. I wanted to be invisible. I wanted to vanish completely. I was sure that Coach would post a notice on the bulletin board or something, I didn't know I'd have to find out right here in front of everybody! I could feel my face getting redder and redder. My head must have looked like a giant cherry tomato. Coach Holt's lips kept moving but I couldn't hear a word he said. Suddenly, Jessica Bergman, the girl sitting beside me, slapped my knee. "Way to go, Brit," she whispered.

I swallowed. Had he really called my name? Relief began to wash over me. My ears opened up and I could hear again. "Tyson, Walker, and Wells. That's it. Thanks for your time, girls." Coach Holt walked back toward the locker room, posting the list of those invited back for the second stage of tryouts.

I couldn't believe I'd made the first cut. Maybe I wasn't that bad after all. When I went into the locker room to change, the sophomores treated with me a new respect. They even made room at the end of one of the benches for me. I couldn't wait to tell Eric and Brian.

We shot hoops outside of Brian's house after tryouts and the boys were more surprised than I was that I got asked back. I guess that says a lot about what they really thought of my ability. After shooting around for awhile I sauntered home, a new confidence in my step. Luckily, I would have some time to work on my dribbling——oh no, piano lessons. I hurried home, anxious to persuade Mom to cancel the lesson. Every moment was important now.

By the time I had breathlessly spilled my news, Mom was shaking her head. "Piano lessons are only a half hour out of your day, Brittany. Besides," she said, getting her car keys, "it's not good to get so focused on one thing at your age."

So that night I resigned myself to sitting still and making my fingers stumble over those awful-sounding scales and classical junk. But the whole time, I couldn't get tryouts, shooting, or basketball out of my mind. The fifth time Mrs. Ripley had me play some stupid Beethoven piece, I let my mind wander back to the court. As I hit each key with my finger, I tried to convince myself that somehow, playing piano was a good agility drill. But sitting there on the bench with old Mrs. Ripley, I just wasn't buying it.

After my lesson, I darted back to Brian's. His dad had put up floodlights, so their driveway was well lit for night hoops. The three of us worked through the darkness on my jump shot and other drills from tryouts. Finally, we sat down on the front steps of Brian's house, exhausted. "If you make the team, Brit, you really owe us," Eric remarked, nimbly holding the ball behind his back, making me challenge for it.

"You got it," I managed to squeak, so tired I could hardly keep my eyes from closing.

The night ended abruptly when Brian's mother opened the front door and peeked out. "Brian, you have a telephone call." With that, he stood up and said goodnight. Just before we left though, I caught him wink over at Eric. I knew what that meant— Susan Ambler was on the phone.

Mom washed my lucky Virginia Beach shirt so I could wear it for tryouts the next day. By the time I got out of physics lab, my ninth-period class, most of the other girls were already on the court shooting. A crowd of older students hung around the open doors to the gym, curiously looking in on the tryout. I spotted Eric in the bunch. He waved encouragingly. *Wow,* I thought to myself, *he actually acknowledged me in front of his friends.*

Coach Holt got the tryouts underway quickly. We went through the same drills as the day before and then he had us run around the court until I was sure I would pass out. I was out of breath and panting, sweat dripping from my face, when, from the corner of my eye, I saw Brian and Susan Ambler join Eric at the open door. I stumbled, but caught myself and kept running. Susan always made me feel clumsy.

Free throws were next. I redid the orange scrunchee holding back my hair. I was letting it grow and it was just a little too short to stay back with ease. Mostly, it hung down in stringy, wet strands on either side of my face. I didn't mind too much. We weren't supposed to be models, we were playing basketball. Still, when I saw Susan Ambler standing there, looking cool and neat with her blonde hair floating over her shoulders, I felt, well, like a total klutz. I tried to put her out of my mind and focus on the free throws. *Calm down, Brit,* I told myself. *Put everything out of your mind but the hoop.*

I shot five free throws and wasn't close on any of them. Something was wrong. I always made my free throws. Susan had rattled me. I chanced a glance over at Coach Holt, who was talking with another one of the girls and trying to help her with her dribbling. I hoped he hadn't seen me throw up those

21

clunkers.

A few minutes later Coach blew the whistle and we took a seat in the bleachers. Up until that last set of free throws, I felt fairly confident. I even thought I'd had a better day today than yesterday. Coach began with the same message as the day before: "At your age a lot can change in a year so don't be too discouraged if you don't make the team." *Yeah right,* I thought to myself.

He cleaned his throat and addressed the pack, "I have to admit, it was really hard deciding, but I did the best I could." He glanced down at the clipboard in his hands. "As for those who didn't make the team, I hope nobody takes it too hard, because every one of you is a winner just for trying."

I offered another sarcastic, "Yeah right," this one loud enough for Tracy Timbers, one of the girls sitting in front of me, to giggle at.

Coach took a deep breath. "If I call your name, I'll look for you here tomorrow afternoon and every afternoon until the season's over."

Goodbye, Mrs. Ripley, I thought to myself, holding my breath and crossing my fingers.

Then Coach began calling names. I had a funny feeling in my stomach. I listened impatiently as he called out all the sophomores who'd played last year. They all made it, no surprise there. I kept listening as he went through the rest of the spots. When he finished speaking, I was motionless. He hadn't called my name. I didn't make the team. My stomach was now feeling really sick and for a minute I thought I was going to lose it, right there in the bleachers. My face felt hot. Everybody in the gym seemed to be staring at me. They were pointing their fingers at me and laughing. I suddenly wished Eric hadn't come, and Brian, and especially Susan Ambler.

All around me, girls were jumping off the bleachers, giving each other high fives, shrieking and hugging. I stumbled down from my seat, still in shock. Quickly, I grabbed my book bag and headed for the exit. Knowing I couldn't face the jubilant crowd in the locker room, I raced out through a side door to the gym and shot down the sidewalk toward home. At first, I hadn't really expected to make the team, but after yesterday, I'd let myself think that maybe I had a chance. Hot tears stung my eyes, but I refused to cry. Somebody might see me and discover how much I actually cared.

It took a while for me to get over my disappointment. At first, I blamed it all on Susan Ambler. She broke my concentration. If she hadn't showed up, fawning all over Brian, I'd have made those baskets and I'd be on the team now. Then I blamed Coach Holt. If he would have been paying attention to me when I made all those free throws that first day, he would have seen what a good player I was. Finally, I just resigned myself to making the team next season.

Naturally, I didn't want anything to do with the girls who made the team. OK, I admit it, I was bitter. But then a couple of them ended up being in my math class and once we got to know each other, I started going to some of their games. Since Eric and Brian were both on the boys' team, they didn't have a lot of time for me, so I kind of got in the habit of cheering for the Jefferson girls' JV.

And when Lindsay Anderson, the team's scorekeeper,

got mono (a really bad version of the flu that lasts like three months), I helped out by keeping the stats. I got to know the players better and learned a lot about the game, too. It didn't take a genius to see that when a player made most of her baskets from a certain point on the court, she ought to concentrate on trying to get open from there. I started seeing the game in a different way. I was noticing passing lanes, I could read what other defenses were doing and knew where the ball had to be and who was the best person to get it to. Most of the girls never thought about basketball this way. Coach Holt called me a natural and said that some day I would make a great coach myself, whatever that meant.

But I didn't want to be a natural or a coach——I wanted to play.

CHAPTER THREE

LAYOVER

"Flight attendants, please prepare for arrival."

I leaned against the window of the plane, gazing at the golden California mountains as they rose up from a bank of fog. San Francisco and a long layover—I would have to kill four hours before my connecting flight to Los Angeles and Olympic trials.

I'd hardly had the chance to catch my breath since Clarissa and I got the word on the tryouts. It seemed that as soon as we stepped up our practices, final exams started. And then we only had a day between the end of finals and graduation. Before I knew it, I was packing my bag for Los Angeles.

The captain's voice brought me back to reality, "The ground temperature here in San Francisco is sixty-eight degrees. It looks like a fair day ahead. We thank you for flying with us today and hope to see you again soon."

Once more I felt a pang of guilt that Clarissa wasn't here with me. I was living out our dream without her. Her Achilles tendon was giving her trouble again and the doctors insisted she skip the trials if she was serious about the WNBA. She desperately wanted to play in the Olympics, but the danger of a career-threatening injury was too great.

I'd never been to San Francisco and had an entire afternoon of sightseeing planned for today. Impatient to start, I fiddled with my seat belt, waiting for the pilot to open the doors of the aircraft. I already had my carry-on bag in hand, carefully turned so everyone I passed would be sure to see the words "'US Olympic Trials'" printed in bold letters on the red, white, and blue bag. I was proud that I had been invited to try out for the team. But being as small as I am, I don't think anyone on that plane thought much about my bag. They probably assumed that I was a trainer or a tourist who'd bought the bag at a gift shop. So much for stardom.

When I entered the main terminal I folded up my San Francisco city map and pushed it into my pocket, heading directly for the baggage lockers. OK, put a couple of quarters in the slot (careful, Brittany, not your lucky Washington one), turn the key, and here we go. Whenever I conversed inside my head, it usually meant that I was nervous.

There's the sign for transportation. I glanced down at my wrist, resetting it to Pacific Standard Time. I walked quickly through a traffic jam of people, while trying to make the adjustment on my watch. I wasn't looking where I was going and someone bumped me so hard that I stumbled across the corridor and slammed into a man at the water fountain.

Flustered, I began to apologize. "I'm sorry I——" My heart stopped.

The young naval officer spoke in a deep voice, "Are you OK?" He picked up my bag, which had fallen to the floor and handed it to me.

I was speechless, too busy staring at the uniform with the brass buttons and the smattering of medals across his chest to get out a word. He was more handsome than I remembered. I was wearing a hat that disguised me fairly well, so I wasn't too upset when Brian didn't recognize me right away. "You know, you remind me of someone I grew up with."

I took my hat off, revealing what Brian had suspected. "Brian," I finally managed to squeak out.

His light blue eyes crinkled and a smile came to his face. "Brittany?" he asked, shaking his head. He laughed in disbelief, looking me up and down. "Is that really you? I haven't seen you since you were eighteen."

I nodded, trying to look older and more composed, even self-assured.

He gave me a quick hug. "Wow, you look great."

"You too. So what are you doing here?" I blurted out nervously.

"Well, flying, obviously." He laughed in that same old slightly sarcastic teasing voice I remembered from childhood. "You?"

"I'm, uh, headed to Los Angeles," I stammered.

"Oh, that's too bad," he said. I heard a glimmer of regret in his voice. "I'm passing through on my way back to Bremerton, Washington. I've got a long layover." He looked

around at the airport terminal fondly. "Great place to be held up, though. San Francisco's just about my favorite city in the world." His blue eyes found me again.

I hesitated, "I actually have a few hours too." I was sure that Brian had a girlfriend and I didn't want to seem pushy. "Do you think you could point me toward the bus, Brian?" I asked politely.

His voice brightened at once. "Well, how about I show you around instead? You always needed a little instruction, anyway." He was awkward when he said, "If you're up for it, I mean."

Was I up for it? Was I ever! I tried to be nonchalant. "I guess. I mean, if you have the time," I shrugged casually.

He snatched up his brown duffel bag and squinted out at the clear blue sky. "Let's see if I can convince the car rental people to let a navy guy have a convertible."

Brian was as good as his word. In no time, we were out of the airport, buckling our seat belts in the front seat of a red Mustang. "This is going to handle a little differently than my jet, but I'll try to keep it under control." He turned the key in the ignition and revved the engine.

"You always wanted to fly, Brian." I laughed, remembering how I could usually steal the ball from him if there was a plane overhead. I got to be very good at picking up the sound of a jet engine because I knew Brian couldn't keep his eyes from straying to the sky.

The summer before my sophomore year at Jefferson High, I spent practically every waking hour with a basketball in my hand. Dad put a hoop up over our garage door and I practiced there every day while Mom nagged me through the kitchen window. "If you just spent a tiny bit of the time you spend on basketball——" she began.

"On the piano?" I continued her sentence, shooting a jumper.

"Well, you'd be so successful, Brit." Mom told me this about ten times a day. If she was trying to make me feel guilty, she did. If she was trying to make me love playing the piano, she was failing. Eventually, just to make her stop talking about it, I'd go in and spend a half hour or so at Gran's piano. I didn't mind the scales, as long as there weren't too many black keys. Those sharps and flats were killers.

Then I turned to the hated Beethoven. With a sigh, I glanced out the open windows, feeling sorry for the neighbors who were being subjected to the stumbling, halting discord that floated from our home. I wanted to try something different but Mrs. Ripley was more determined than a three-legged dog. She insisted that I memorize this stupid Beethoven piece if it was the last thing I did. As the summer wore on, I was beginning to think it might be.

Before I knew it, school started up again. Eric and Brian were juniors that year, so they were pretty busy with upperclassmen stuff. But we still played basketball every afternoon. I could tell I was getting better, especially since I'd figured out where my shot was. Now I'm not saying I was Theresa Witherspoon or anything, but I was improving. I liked spotting up from the top of the key, even with Eric and Brian in my face. I practiced this shot all the time until it was nearly unstoppable. Sometimes late at night I would do push-ups and sit-ups. And occasionally, if I was feeling really motivated, I would even lift some of Eric's weights. So I was much faster and stronger than a year earlier. And thanks or no thanks to piano lessons, my hands were very, very quick.

When October rolled around and JV tryouts were held again, I had a better idea of what to expect. For one thing, I knew not to get my hopes up. And because of my off-season preparation, I entered the tryout with a newfound confidence. I walked with my chin up, passed with ferocity, and ran Coach Holt's drills as if I'd been practicing them all summer. The truth was, I had been.

After we did some standard drill-type stuff, Coach threw us a curve. He divided us up into four teams for a series of one-quarter games. This was totally unexpected, and while all the girls stood around pretending not to look one another over, Coach Holt introduced four guys from the boys' varsity team. They would be our squad coaches for the day. I lucked out here, because Brian volunteered to coach team two, the one I was on. When he told me I'd be playing point guard, I didn't argue. Now I don't want to give you the impression that I did everything Brian told me to do. It just so happens that point guard was the position I wanted to play and the one Coach Holt had told me I had "the right brain" for.

Coach threw us some old team jerseys to put on over our own shirts. Our team got the red ones. (Another stroke of luck—red's my favorite color.)

When he blew his whistle to start play, I was really nervous and had a hard time keeping my palms from sweating.

One of the girls on my squad, Kendra Grant, had been on the JV team last year and was their leading scorer. My strategy was to toss the ball from my sweaty palms to her dry ones as often as possible. I knew that a good point guard got the ball to her best scorers in positions where they had the best opportunity to score. This was the simple philosophy I tried to let play out on the floor.

It took a few runs up and down the court before anybody settled down enough to make a shot. I thought I was doing OK, holding my own, seeing the open player and making sharp passes. But in no time, Coach's whistle sounded and the next set of players took the court.

I started to relax on the bench, but Brian gave me the eye. "Keep your head in the game, Brit." So I sat up straight, paying as close attention as I would have if I'd been keeping the stats. I tried to get an overview of the game. I noticed some players that were real ball hogs——no surprise, every team and every pick-up game anywhere has their share. I saw others who were afraid of touching the ball, probably for fear of making a mistake. There were even a few who seemed more concerned with not breaking a fingernail than with catching the ball. Now, nobody likes the hottest color in nails more than I do, but basketball and long fingernails just don't mix. (Mrs. Ripley, my piano teacher, says the same thing, but I admit it's easier for me to give up the nice nails for basketball than Beethoven.) I had an entire life ahead of me to grow pretty fingernails. Right now, the game was what mattered most.

There were just five minutes left when Coach blew his whistle and told the boys to send out a few players from each group. This time, I wasn't surprised when Brian told me that I was the point guard. This was my natural position, and I knew from that day forward that if I was playing basketball anywhere, I was playing point guard.

I controlled the ball and dribbled confidently, head up, eyes perusing the court. Kendra was posted up with her back to the basket and I quickly fired a pass at her hands. Like she was reading my mind, she grabbed it and put it in all in one motion.

The other players brushed by me as they raced back down toward our goal. I held up just in front of the half-court line and put some pressure on the guard bringing the ball up. Now I may have been the smallest one on the floor, but I was smart and scrappy. I'd seen how the tiniest bit of heat made her uneasy, so I came at her like a wildfire. Out of control, she forced an entry pass in down low. We intercepted her effort easily. There was no way she was getting that one in there. I brought the ball back up-court and faked a shot from beyond the three-point arc. The moment Sharon Nichols fell for it, leaving her feet and leaping into the air, I tossed a bounce pass inside to Kendra again. She put it up off the window and was fouled in the process. Nobody used the backboard quite like Kendra. Although the basket counted, she missed her free throw. The errant shot ricocheted hard off the side of the rim and Ann, a player from the other team, grabbed the rebound, looking up-court right away. Their center was waiting under the basket for the long outlet pass. But I read Ann's eyes and reached high into the air, my fingers barely managing to tip the long pass. The ball skipped off my fingertips and right into Kendra's hands. She nailed another ten-footer off the window. Her basket capped off my best five minutes of the tryouts, especially defensively.

When the whistle blew, we grabbed some water and sat down to watch the next two teams collide. But our game turned out to be the last game——the tryout was over. My heart nearly jumped out of my chest when Coach Holt called us together. We all knew that the first cut was coming.

I was pretty sure I'd make it. No, I was sure. I wasn't sure that I'd make the team, but I was certain I was better than at least half the girls there. This time, I was right.

I raced home, finished my homework, and was at Brian's house by the time he and Eric got there. Fortunately, it wasn't Monday, so I didn't have a piano lesson. "You looked pretty good out there, Brit," Brian spoke, smiling. He slapped Eric on the back. "You'd have been impressed, man."

Eric rolled his eyes and hit me in the back of the head with the basketball when I wasn't looking.

I had a free period before tryouts the next day, so I lounged around the gym, taking an occasional warm-up shot. My hair had gotten longer and Kendra braided it for me so it wasn't constantly falling out of the scrunchee and hanging in my eyes.

"We've been talking about the whole team braiding red, white and blue beads into our hair for the season," Kendra confided as she neatly tied the end of a braid.

I sighed, not sure what to say. I didn't want to jinx myself. Kendra knew what I was thinking and grinned. "Come on, Brittany, you're going to make it. You know that, don't you?"

Before I could answer, Brian walked up, "I found this on the sidewalk." He held out a quarter in the palm of his hand. "It just came out, it's the Washington one." He flipped it to me, "Maybe it'll bring you luck."

"Just don't put it in your shoe," Kendra warned.

I slipped the quarter in my pocket and went out onto the court. Kendra and I took turns shooting free throws until Coach Holt arrived and started putting us through the skill drills again. We were down to half the girls we'd had yesterday and he still put each of us through two quarters of play. Brian wasn't coaching my squad today, but when asked what position I wanted, I chose point guard, the playmaker slot. I had another good day of tryouts, playing smart basketball: no turnovers and no crazy shots.

When it was time for the team to be selected, I would have been feeling really good about my chances if what happened last year hadn't still been so fresh in my mind. I took an inconspicuous seat in the back row, not wanting to be seen slithering away in the event that I did get cut. Across the gym, Brian gave me a thumbs up and I rubbed the quarter in my pocket for good luck. I tried not to think about what was about to take place.

But this time, everything worked out, and after a year of waiting, "Brittany Bristol ..."

I shot out of my seat like a rocket the moment my name was called. When Coach Holt stopped talking, there was yelling and screaming and whoops of joy all around me. Somewhere in the background, I heard him remind us to be back here tomorrow after last period. I was on the team.

Caught up in my good fortune, I could think of nothing else. I floated to the locker room, gathered up my things, and headed out to the main hallway, hoping to see Brian. I saw him all right, standing in a corner locking lips with Susan Ambler. He didn't even look up, but I wasn't about to let that spoil my day.

I don't think my feet touched the ground all the way home. Racing into the kitchen, I bounded into Mom's arms. I didn't have to tell her what happened. She took one look at me and knew immediately. "Congratulations!" she exclaimed.

My expression changed, "Of course, I'll have practice every day after school, so I guess we'll have to call Mrs. Ripley."

"And reschedule your piano lessons," Mom finished my sentence.

"Mom," I began, certain that the whine in my voice would telegraph the meaning.

"Remember what you promised when we got Gran's piano?"

"How can I forget?"

Mom put the telephone to her ear and dialed, "Do you prefer Saturday mornings or early evenings?"

CHAPTER FOUR

LOSING IT

I sat comfortably in the front seat, leaning my right arm out the window so my body was positioned facing Brian. I didn't tell him, but this was my first time in a convertible. Besides the tricks it played with my hair, I liked it.

"How's Eric?" Brian asked, as we pulled onto the San Francisco freeway.

I answered after a short delay, "He's good. Just got accepted to vet school at Ohio College. He starts in the fall. Must be Mad Max's influence," I laughed, remembering Brian's wild terrier.

He smiled at the thought of Max. "Remember the time he chewed up Jimmy Bower's kicking tee and Jimmy chased him like three miles?"

I giggled, "Yeah, I don't think Jim ever forgave you, either."

"I loved that dog." Brian stared off for a second. *"Is Eric still seeing——um, what was her name?" he prodded. "You know who I mean, the cheerleader, the one with the blonde hair."*

"Susan Ambler," I supplied, none too pleased to be reminded of her. *"I'm surprised you could forget her, Brian. The two of you were practically inseparable."*

"Until she decided she liked your brother." He laughed, unaffected. After all, from what I'd heard, Brian replaced Susan with darling Starling.

"Fortunately for Eric, they're no longer a couple." I hope my voice didn't sound too bitter. *"He's seeing a girl he met at college, but I don't think it's too serious."* I was dying to know about Brian's love life, but I tried to keep my voice casual. *"And you? Are you still seeing Sherry Sterling?"* Now this was the million dollar question. I tried not to blush, but had a hard time hiding my feelings for Sherry.

Brian noticed how uncomfortable I'd just gotten. *"You never liked Sherry much, did you?"* he asked.

I couldn't lie to him, *"Well, not really."*

"She's a great girl, just misunderstood. Boy has she had it rough." Yeah right, I thought, not knowing how to respond. I got quiet, guessing that Brian was still seeing Sherry. Too bad, I thought, Brian and I are really good together. Brian broke into my thoughts, grinning. *"To answer your question— I'm single. Sailors don't settle down that easily."*

"So you're not dating Sherry?" I needed a confirmation here.

"No," he said. I cracked a small smile, half confused,

half delighted. "Anyway," he changed the subject, "you were about to tell me why you're headed to LA."

I tried to keep the pride from my voice when I said, "Olympic trials at Los Angeles State."

"No kidding?" Brian looked shocked. "Wow! Good for you, Brit!" He gave a low whistle. "I had no idea you were that good."

"I'm not really," I said modestly.

"And you're so little, too. You must have a heck of a jumper, huh?"

"I'm OK," I confessed.

"Well, you must be pretty great to get invited to try out for the Olympics. That's something else, Brit." Brian was definitely impressed.

He turned his attention back to the traffic as the city loomed in front of us. I dug out my camera and snapped away while he looked for a parking space.

"The first thing you have to do in San Francisco is take a cable car ride," Brian advised.

I couldn't deny the thrill of excitement as I looked at the red cable cars climbing up the steep hills. I guess it was the hills that jogged my memory and I started to laugh.

"What's so funny?" Brian looked mystified.

"Remember the time you had your Dad's car on Skyline Drive?" The image of Eric, myself, and a couple of other kids packed into that station wagon as it rolled downhill was as clear as if it happened yesterday.

"Yeah, I got on the wrong road giving you a ride home from piano lessons. Then I ran out of gas. Nice memory, Brit."

Brian groaned.

Fortunately, my piano lessons were switched to early Wednesday evenings, which worked out as well as could be expected. We had practice in the gym on Mondays and Thursdays, while the guys had the gym on Tuesdays and Fridays. I was probably the busiest fifteen-year-old girl on the planet. After basketball practice, I'd race home, do my homework, practice the piano and eat dinner before rushing back to school for either my game or Eric's.

Despite my busy schedule, I played hard, giving everything I had each afternoon. I guess I shouldn't have expected to start right away, but my feelings were hurt when I didn't get to. What made things worse for me was the fact that Christine Davis, the girl who started in front of me, hardly ever missed a minute of a game. So by December, I was fairly accustomed to sitting on the bench.

Being on the sidelines made analyzing our games easier. My conclusion at the halfway point of our season was that we were simply too selfish out there. The concept of "team" was constantly adjusted depending on who was on the floor at the time. This was true off the court as well. Despite the fact that Kendra had been really friendly to me at tryouts, once the season got underway, she tended to pal around with the other starters. The bad news continued when I discovered the red, white, and blue beads were just for the first team, not the back-ups. I tried not to care, but it was hard. All five starters were sophomores, my classmates. I was the only non-freshman on the team who wasn't in the starting lineup. This made me feel even more awkward.

One Wednesday, Christine, the starting point guard, wasn't at school for the first three periods. She came in later, but Coach Holt's rule was that if you weren't in school all day, you didn't play. No exceptions. As it turned out, Christine felt better as the day went on and made it to school by fifth period, fully expecting to start that afternoon. Coach wasn't having it, and told her right away that she couldn't dress for the game.

We were playing against our rival from Shenandoah in a crucial conference contest. My chance to play had finally arrived. I was going to be in the starting lineup. Shenandoah took the floor first as the visiting team, and then we raced out in our red warm ups. I tried to stay calm and under control, telling myself that this was a game like any other. But that wasn't close to the truth. This was a game like no other. The difference with this game was that today I was on the hardwood floor, not the bench.

By tip-off, I was a bag of nerves, and I bobbled the first ball that was passed to me. It skittered off my foot and slammed against the bleachers. Out of bounds. *Way to start the game off, Brit.*

Shenandoah took the inbounds pass and I got set to cover their wiry and explosive guard, Sherry Sterling. It was the first time I had ever seen Sherry, and this was the beginning of our rivalry. As I reached out to disrupt her dribble, she flicked the ball behind her back, changing direction, and leaving me off balance one minute and flat on my back the next. I had never defended such a skilled ball handler. She scored easily before I got to my feet again.

Audrey passed the ball to me and my heart pounded so loudly I could hear it over the bouncing of the ball, the crowd, and Coach Holt's screaming. I was determined to make up for my early mistakes and fired a hard pass over to Kendra. The ball was too high and bounced off her hands, out of bounds.

Coach quickly called a time-out.

In the huddle, I could tell by the scowl on his face that he was upset. "Settle down, Brit, you've got way too much adrenaline."

Kendra and Audrey both glared at me. Down at the end of the bench, Christine, not dressed for the game, rolled her eyes and sighed. I took a quick swig of water and resolved to do better.

I struggled to keep it simple for the rest of the half, bringing the ball up-court and feeding it to Kendra and Audrey. This strategy was working and we managed to get through that first half tied.

Still, in the locker room, I couldn't miss the cold shoulder I was getting from the other players. I overheard Coach Holt telling Kendra that it was up to my teammates to "help Brittany along out there." I almost wished I was back on the bench and out of the spotlight.

The buzzer for the second half sounded and we took the floor again. Sterling came out really hot. In fact, she was virtually unstoppable. Coach Holt put two of us on their sharp-shooter and still we couldn't contain her. Finally, he looked at me desperately, "Come on Brit, make a play. You can do it." His words inspired me, if only for the moment.

Kendra rolled her eyes disdainfully, but I was pretty

sure Coach was right, I could do *something*. I was certain that I'd worked my jitters out by now. So the next time Shenandoah brought the ball up-court, I put myself between Sherry and the basket. She took the pass and began to dribble by me, but I reached out and caught a piece of the ball. It tipped high into the air, where Kendra grabbed it. With nothing between her and the basket, it was an easy layup. I did the exact same thing the next time they came down the court and could feel the excitement begin to build. Yeah, I was the shortest girl on the court, and I didn't have the best shot either, but I could make things happen and I was starting to show everyone in the arena just that. We scored another layup and had finally built some momentum.

I started to feel confident, so on the very next play, when Sherry Sterling took the pass and dribbled toward me, I reached my fingers out again. This time, however, I didn't get the ball. Somehow, I lost my balance and went sprawling across the floor, knocking both Kendra and Audrey to the ground. Sherry leaped over us, driving to the basket and scoring easily. Everyone in the gym seemed to be laughing at the three of us on the floor.

I dribbled up the court and fired a pass into Kendra, who missed an easy shot from about three feet away. Shenandoah roared away on another fast break. They were up by four now. We had to do something to keep the game close.

When Sherry drove the lane on the next play I was certain that I had a good position. My feet weren't moving and I'd established the fact that I was standing there before her, so the ref would have to call a charging foul if she barreled me over.

I stood my ground and Sherry jumped into the air, colliding

directly into my chest. The referee's whistle blew and I clapped my hands enthusiastically, waiting for him to make the right call. But my ears couldn't believe what they heard. He was calling a blocking foul on me!

Right away, I ran over to him, spreading my arms wide and doing something Coach Holt warned us never, ever, to do. I talked back to the ref. "A foul?" I said, incredulous. "Are you blind? That's the worst call I've ever seen. She charged right over me!"

Just as I finished my tirade the whistle blew again. Technical foul.

My face flamed as Kendra shoved me toward the bench in a hostile way. I could hear Eric groan from far up in the stands. I didn't dare look at Coach Holt, as I took a seat as far down the bench as I could get. He sent in Sheila McCoy, one of the freshman guards, to replace me. She stayed in for the rest of the game, managing not to do anything wrong.

Although we still couldn't stop Shenandoah's Sherry Sterling, Kendra got hot. She began to light up the scoreboard from about ten feet out. Sheila and Audrey fed her the ball every trip down the floor. It was like magic. Kendra would fake from fifteen feet out and then duck under the coverage and toss it up from ten. And if they gave her a few steps, she'd fade back and bury shot after shot. She managed to outjump, outshoot, outrebound, and outplay the entire Shenendoah team.

We got the win, a six-point victory that I should have been happy about. But I was mortified. I knew the other girls thought they'd won in spite of me. I showered and dressed quickly, attempting to leave the locker room before anyone else.

On my way out, everyone pointedly ignored me. But just before I reached the exit, Coach Holt called me into his office. I had no choice but to go in.

"Close the door, Brittany." He sounded reasonably calm. "Sit down." He tossed his pencil on the desk and wheeled around to look me in the eye. "Want to tell me what happened out there?"

I shrugged, "I guess I just lost it. I know we're not supposed to say anything to the refs, it just slipped out. I'm sorry." I looked down at my hands clenched into fists in my lap. "I know I didn't play well."

"You don't have a lot of game experience, Brit, and that can't help but show. Still, you played hard. And I would have left you in, but I just couldn't after that technical. If I don't send a message that I don't tolerate that kind of thing, well, everybody will be doing it."

I nodded, on the verge of tears.

His voice became quiet. "The girls gave you a hard time out there too, huh?"

"Can't say that I blame them," I responded with a tear rolling down my cheek.

"It isn't easy breaking into a unit that has played together. If you're not a hotshot, you're not readily accepted. And if you are a hotshot, everybody's jealous of you." He tossed me a bottle of water. "This is a funny game, basketball. Keep at it though, Brit. You'll find that balance."

I left his office and Eric was waiting for me outside. "Tough break."

I knew I must have looked awful if Eric was being so nice

to me. "Where's Brian?" I asked, hoping to change the subject.

"Begging Susan to take him back," he replied, laughing.

"What'd he do?" If anything could have cheered me up right then, it was the thought of Brian and Susan Ambler breaking up.

"Nothing, she's just tired of him, I guess."

"So who's her new victim?" I didn't bother to hide my disgust.

Eric stumbled over the edge of the curb. "Don't know," he mumbled and starting walking faster.

I didn't see much more playing time during the rest of the year, although I got into games late in the fourth quarter when we were ahead by enough. After finishing tied for first place in the conference, we faced off with Shenendoah once again. This final game would determine the better team and we were all psyched.

Shenandoah had a new gym with state-of-the-art loudspeakers and all sorts of fancy stuff. When the home team was announced, they put out all the lights and let each player run into a spotlight. I have to say, it was awesome. I wondered if I would ever get a chance to play in college, maybe have my name called in a spotlight.

The odds were stacked against us that day. We came in with three of our starting players getting over the flu and the other two beginning to show symptoms. Plus, we were accustomed to playing in a regular gym with folding bleachers and not much in the way of refreshments. So we were a little intimidated by Shenandoah's gym. The last thing we needed was Sherry Sterling getting a hot hand.

Once the game started, that's exactly what we got. Sherry picked up right where she'd left off in our gym, swishing nearly every shot she took. We plugged away the best we could through three quarters, but by the fourth, the starters were worn out and Coach Holt called for me and Sheila to go in. We gave it all we had, and I got aggressive on defense, managing to steal the ball three or four times. I only fouled once, when I caught Sterling's wrist by accident. You can bet that I put my hand up quickly to signal that I had committed the foul. And I kept my mouth shut this time too.

Toward the end of the fourth quarter, Shenandoah put all their subs in and the game got a little rough. I was fouled several times and ended up making all ten of my free throws. So, I had a decent game. It was only the second time that season I'd played more than a few minutes. Anyway, despite my decent game, we lost by fifteen points. Needless to say, the bus ride home was as silent as sleep.

CHAPTER FIVE

COACH JENSEN

"You still like Chinese food?" Brian asked, as we stepped off the cable car in San Francisco's Chinatown.

"Still my favorite. I'm surprised you remembered."

We walked across a crowded street and he placed his hand on my back to steer me through. This was a different hand than I remembered from childhood, a stronger and more experienced one. I admit, his touch gave me a thrill. I squinted up at him in the sun. I think he was a few inches taller now too.

"So did you ever learn how to use chopsticks?" he teased as we turned down a little alley, walking past some older Chinese men who were doing Tai Chi exercises in the park.

"I did, actually." I was a little embarrassed, recalling how Brian used to be over at our house when Dad would order Chinese (usually on nights where Mom had a PTA meeting or something). Brian and Eric picked right up on the chopsticks

when Dad showed them how. Not me. I used to drop half my food on my shirt. Dad would try to hand me a fork, but I insisted on being like the boys. I can't imagine how silly I must have looked back then. In college, I finally got the knack for chopsticks with some help from Ming.

A moment later we walked into a little restaurant with Chinese lanterns out front.

"Hang Ah Tearoom," Brian explained. "I used to come here all the time. Sometimes we'd port in San Francisco for the night. This is where I'd have dinner."

Brian's stories were fascinating to me. He'd traveled all over the country, all over the world! My eyes peeled off of him as an elderly man set plates of hot dumplings in front of us. Even though I was a chopstick expert, I had a vision of that slippery dumpling sitting on my lap, instead of in my mouth.

"You get to San Francisco often, then?" I inquired, popping a potsticker expertly into my mouth with the chopsticks.

"My roommate at the Naval Academy was from here. We're both stationed at Bremerton, across Puget Sound from Seattle." He bit into an egg roll. "So what are you going to do now that you're out of college?" He nodded toward my camera case. "Win the Pulitzer Prize?"

"Maybe," I grinned. "I definitely want to give photography a try. Unless——" My voice trailed off.

"Unless what?"

My heart beat a little faster as I confessed my dream to Brian, "I'd like to try and walk onto a WNBA team. Does that sound crazy?"

He got serious for a second, "No way, that sounds

great."

I don't know if it was his easy smile or just the way he spoke, but Brian was exactly as I remembered him—and more. I poured another cup of tea. There was a serious silence that Brian finally broke, "I wonder what Eric would think of this."

"Think of what?" I asked.

Brian took a sip of water. "Me and you, hanging out."

"Why would Eric care?" I was confused.

Brian laughed, "He wouldn't. Not now at least. It's just that—you know he used to give me such a hard time about you. Talk about an overprotective brother."

"Eric?" I asked.

"Oh yeah, he was impossible. I always wanted to ask you out during high school, but Eric was just too much." Did Brian just say that he always wanted to ask me out? This news was absolutely shocking to me. Brian continued, "I used to bug Eric all the time—eventually it was just a running joke. 'Hey, when you're not looking, I'm going to ask Brittany out.'"

So my whole life, Brian wanted to date me and Eric told him I was off limits. I'll kill him, I thought. But then a smile came to my face and suddenly I wanted to call my older brother and thank him for looking after me.

I looked at Brian, "I don't know what to say, except," I paused, wanting to tell him how I was always in love with him and that we should have been together this whole time. Instead, I blurted out, "Eric's not looking anymore."

I worked at the library to earn tuition money for basketball camp at Tennessee College the summer before my junior year of high school. I spent long hours putting children's picture books back onto the shelves, only to have them torn right back out by peanut butter–smeared fingers. Sometimes I wondered if it was worth it, especially with Eric and Brian life guarding at the pool.

While they basked in the sun, I spent my days quietly reading basketball books. By the time August rolled around, I'd read every hoop book in that library and was itching to take my newfound knowledge onto the court. I had just celebrated my sixteenth birthday in August when I headed to Tennessee for basketball camp. I couldn't have been more excited. Camps made a big difference in improving skills and I knew that if I wanted to make varsity next year, I'd need to get much better.

I stepped off the plane in Knoxville, and the sultry summer heat nearly set my face on fire. I could feel the hot sizzle of steam on the sidewalks and was more than glad to find that my dorm was air conditioned. My tour of campus was amazing. I stopped and stared open-mouthed at the gigantic aquatic center with its multiple swimming pools. Hundreds of kids were swimming and sunning beside the cool blue water. If this was college, I couldn't wait.

During my two weeks in Knoxville, we went from drills to technique sessions, to playmaking lectures, to games. We used the few off moments we had at the pool. We were like robots, going from meal to practice to pool to meal. We were so tired that we collapsed into bed at nine o'clock every night and didn't open our eyes until the counselors rousted us at six for early morning runs around the track.

I didn't know what ached most, my legs or my arms, but by the time I boarded the plane back to Washington, I knew I was a much better player. I found out that I had reserves of strength I never even dreamed of.

On the plane ride back to D.C. I thought a lot about college. Where did I want to go? What did I want to study? These were tough questions that I didn't have answers to. At least I decided on one thing, though: When I did eventually go to college I was going to attend a smaller school than Tennessee College.

A few months later I was lacing up my sneakers for tryouts. There was one big difference this year in Coach Holt's tryouts—there was no Coach Holt. He had taken a new job at a junior college and was off to North Carolina. When I stepped into the gym I prepared myself for a meeting with the new girls' basketball coach. This was the worst news I could have gotten that morning. I knew Coach Holt, and was sure he would see my improvements and offer me a spot on varsity. But I wasn't sure what to make of our new coach. She didn't know me, or what I was capable of. *Hey, I might look tiny, but I can play this game,* I thought. Because my game wasn't filled with flash, I wasn't sure how I could prove to her that I was valuable.

Coach Jensen introduced herself. She was young, probably only a few years out of school, and pretty too, with long blonde hair and a perfect smile. She opened the tryouts by saying she would be doing some things differently. What that meant, none of us knew. "There'll be a couple of new twists this year," Coach Jensen spoke in a soft voice, and unlike the rest of us, without any trace of a Southern accent. "For one thing, I'm holding the varsity and JV tryouts together." A confused

51

groan went up from the crowd, but only the upperclassmen among the crowd. I could sense a rush of excitement among the freshmen and sophomores, who now had a chance to make the varsity squad. Coach Jensen continued, "And once the rosters are decided, there may be some give and take. A player will not necessarily stay on the same team all season. There's room for improvement."

"And screwing up," Kendra said sarcastically.

"I've divided you up into teams of five. These teams will change daily, so check the bulletin board in the locker room first thing and pick up a jersey with the appropriate color. We'll run quarter-long games for the first four days of tryouts, then the last day, we'll do some shooting, passing, and defensive drills." Five days of tryouts? "To make today a little easier we'll begin with the seniors and move down. You'll play by classes." She blew a whistle. "Hit the floor!"

Kendra and I scrambled down to the far court for warm ups, racing to round up stray balls while the rest of the juniors followed. The freshmen and sophomores kind of stumbled around, trying to find a place to practice while the seniors played. Naturally, we took the lion's share of balls and hoops.

When it came time for the juniors to take the court for a scrimmage, I did OK. I got a few steals and made a couple of defensive plays. But I didn't take any shots on offense. Instead, I tried to concentrate on what I did best: playing defense and getting the ball to the open player. I hoped this would be enough.

The next four days passed pretty quickly. I gave the tryouts all I had and the confidence I'd built up at summer camp served me well. Until, of course, the witching hour. Despite doing things differently, Coach Jensen's "sorry you got cut" speech sounded exactly like Coach Holt's. "I hope you'll all accept the results with good sportsmanship. Unfortunately, there wasn't room for every one of you on a team. Thank you for coming out and trying, the list will be posted on Monday morning."

Over the weekend, I tried to focus on other things, but it was like trying to ignore the elephant in the room. I played the piano a lot (something I never did voluntarily), and it momentarily took my attention away from basketball. Mom never smiled so brightly. Playing the piano was all I could do to stop myself from biting my fingernails right off my hands. I was a nervous wreck. I don't think I slept a wink Sunday night before the list was posted. I tossed and turned in my bed, wondering if my name would appear on it.

At breakfast Monday morning I tried to figure out when the best time to check the list was. Should I go in early, late, or after the class bell rings? I wanted to look when nobody else was around. As I dawdled over Mom's pancakes, Eric must have figured out what I was thinking.

"You want me to check the list for you, Brit?" he offered.

"Do you mind?" I said at once, surprised by my brother's kindness. Then I took hold of myself. If I was too scared to look at the stupid list, I was too scared to play on the team. "Actually, no. I guess I should," I amended, trying to be brave.

"Look, Brit, even if you don't make the team, it's not the end of the world." Eric was trying hard to be nice about this. Who was this guy? "Brian and I will still shoot hoops with you. We don't care if you're on varsity or not. And hey," he grinned, "you'll never be as good as us anyway so don't worry about it."

Now that sounded more like the Eric I knew.

"In your dreams, Eric," I said dismissing his comment. I took one more bite of my pancakes and left the house early. I had to get to school——to that list.

When I approached the bulletin board, there were a few kids standing down at the far end of the hall. They didn't pay any attention to me, so I sidled up closer and scanned the names. "Ramirez, O'Connell, James, Washington, Conners, Ochoa, Price, Johnson, Heap. So far, no surprise, they were all a lock," I whispered to myself, reading on. "Andrews, Mayfield, Long, Chen, Smith, Short."

My eyes went back to the top of the list. I read it again and lowered my head. I didn't make it. A big lump settled in my chest and stomach, a lump so big I almost couldn't breathe. I guess I wasn't that surprised, but I'd worked so hard. If only Coach Holt were still here, I told myself, my name would have been on that list.

As I turned to walk away, Marilyn called to me, "Brit, wait up." She hurried over, "So?" she said expectantly. "Are you going to play?"

"Obviously not," I said, trying to keep the bitterness out of my voice.

"No, I mean on junior varsity."

I just looked at her. I didn't have the foggiest idea what she was talking about.

"She put you, Kara, and Lisa on JV. They're in the math lab trying to decide what to do."

"JV?" My voice squeaked. Like I didn't believe her or something. I double checked the board. "Unbelievable," I whispered, "three juniors on JV?"

"And a freshman and two sophomores on varsity," she pointed out.

I raced over to the math lab in time to find Kara and Lisa leaving and Lisa was dabbing at her eyes with a tissue. As bad as I felt, Lisa had taken an even bigger fall. She'd been a starter all last season on JV and fully expected to make varsity without trouble.

"That's it. I've had it!" She sobbed. "Nobody plays JV ball as a junior."

"I don't know how she can do this to us." Kara whined. "Well, she can't force me to play. Let her find somebody else. I quit."

"Me, too." Lisa added, then looked at me. "What about you, Brit?"

"I guess so." This was all happening too fast.

"Then let's go tell her," Kara said, dragging Lisa and me by the arm toward the gym.

"Wait, I can't——not now," I protested, "I have an English test first period."

"You chickening out?" Kara accused, her eyes burning with anger.

"I have a test. I'll tell her later." I shot Kara an annoyed look and left them, heading for English.

I had a really busy day, so it was just after last period when I had time to see Coach Jensen and give her the word that I wouldn't play JV ball.

I knocked on her half-open door, "Coach Jensen," I began.

She leaned back in her chair and regarded me skeptically. "Sit down."

Reluctantly, I did. When I started to speak, my heart nearly jumped out of my chest, across the table, and into Coach Jensen's lap. "I——"

She grabbed a basketball and handed it to me. "Hold this, it'll relax you." I held the ball in my lap and suddenly felt a little less angry. "Feel a little better?" She spoke with a soft kindness behind her words. Despite her cutting me from the varsity team, there was something really likable about Coach Jensen. "You're a junior, too, aren't you, Brittany? So I suppose you're here to tell me you won't play on the JV team, either."

I rolled the ball around in my lap. "That's about the size of it," I conceded.

"You want to tell me why?" she asked. "Kara and Lisa were in such a state all they could do was rant and rave. You impress me as a little steadier."

I shrugged.

"OK, Brittany, I admit that I'm new here at Jefferson, and I understand now that I've ruffled some feathers. I can assure you, I didn't mean to."

"Well, in the past, freshmen and sophomores played junior varsity," I explained, "and upperclassmen made up the varsity. It's the way it's always been here."

"That's the way my high school system operated too, and no one ever questioned it. But I think there's a better way. When I was at Salem State, we ran things the way I'd like to run them here. There are a lot of advantages to an open system for the team and for the players."

"I don't see how it's an advantage for a junior to play on JV." I was forceful in my retort and felt guilty. But the words were out of my mouth before I could take them back.

She smiled. "Would you be surprised to learn that even seniors play JV ball some places?"

I shot her an incredulous look.

"It's true. Sometimes it's better for a girl to play at a level where she can actually see substantial playing time. Sitting on the bench is not the best way to develop."

"But if I was any good, I'd have made the varsity team," I protested.

"You're a playmaking guard, Brittany, and you need to play to refine your skills. Frankly, you're not going to get the playing time on varsity this year. That's the long and short of it." She paused and fiddled with the purple gel pen on her desk. Then she leaned in closer, "A season of playing, and I mean starting, will do wonders for you." She tossed the pen aside. "I was a point guard just like you, I can help you get better, Brit. But you won't see the minutes on varsity. I see something special in you, that's why I did this."

I turned away but could feel her still looking at me. She was making a lot of sense. Playing and starting would do my game a lot of good. But still, there was one thought in my head overpowering the rest, I'm a junior, and juniors don't play JV.

The purple gel pen tapped on the desk one last time. I took a deep breath. "Maybe I should think about it."

She smiled and nodded. "That's great. Go home and sleep on it." She stood up. "You can let me know in the morning."

I nodded.

"And Brittany, think for yourself. Don't let your friends influence you. You have to do what's right for you."

I thought about this choice all the way home. Over dinner, I finally told Mom, Dad, and Eric what Coach Jensen had said to me, not that I really wanted to discuss it. I just toyed with my food, too upset to eat Dad's famous lasagna.

Between mouthfuls, Eric jumped to my defense. "It's not really quitting, you know. She didn't try out for the JV, she tried out for varsity."

"You're right," Mom agreed. "It's up to Brittany to decide what she wants to do."

"Sometimes," Dad interjected, "when I have a tough call to make, I sit down with a piece of paper and make two lists: one list of the advantages and one of the disadvantages. Helps me to see things in black and white." He took a large bite of lasagna, "Mmm, this lasagna is great." We all laughed. Dad rarely cooked, but when he did, he always offered plenty of food and plenty of compliments——to himself.

Later that night, I tried making a list. On the good side, I would get to do something I liked and I'd be a starter. On the bad side, there was some humiliation associated with being a junior on JV. By the time I was finished with both lists, I had filled up a full page in my English notebook. There were five good reasons I should play and only four reasons I shouldn't. Not exactly an overwhelming victory for JV hoops. Still though, I knew what I had to do.

The next morning, I found Coach Jensen in her office before classes started. "Do you have a minute?" I asked, standing at the door.

"Sure, Brittany, come in. Did you make up your mind?"

"Yes. I'll do it, I'll play."

She smiled and reached out to shake my hand. "I don't think you'll be sorry. Lisa came by earlier and she'd like to play, too." She slid an equipment catalog toward me. "I thought we'd order new warm ups this year." She smiled. "As a player, I always thought it might be a good idea if someone actually consulted the people who wear these things before they were ordered. I've marked three or four I thought might be possibilities. Will you and Lisa look them over and let me know what you think?"

My decision was suddenly looking a lot better. I wouldn't be the only junior on the team and Coach Jensen even asked our opinion about things. I strolled off toward English thumbing through the catalog and not paying a whole lot of attention to where I was going. That's probably why I ran smack into Susan Ambler, causing her to drop her baton into the janitor's mop bucket, splashing dirty water all over her lavender blouse.

"You are so graceful, Brittany," Susan spat out, looking helplessly at Eric, who good-naturedly fished her baton out of the smelly bucket.

For a minute, my face started to get all hot and red. Then I realized how really upset Susan was over something so silly. She looked like she might burst into tears. "Sorry," I managed to mumble, trying not to snicker.

I walked away and there was Brian, laughing by his locker, just a few feet away. "Did you do that on purpose?" he asked, knowing perfectly well I did not.

"Now what do you think?" I said, rolling my eyes, grateful that he found Susan's plight amusing.

"That green shirt——it looks good on you. It matches your eyes," he said. I was speechless. You couldn't have convinced me he even knew what color my eyes were. Brian touched the edge of my shirtsleeve and then quickly let go when Eric's eyes met his from across the hallway. As we turned toward the cafeteria, Brian hesitated a minute. "Are you going to Marilyn's birthday party Friday night?"

"Yes." I couldn't imagine why he was asking me that.

"Good. I'll see you there." He started to head into history class.

"Brian? You'll see me before then. Unless you guys are uninviting me to afternoon hoops today."

The normally unflappable Brian flushed a little pink. "Yeah, I mean no, that's not what I meant. You know, I'll see you at the party too."

That was weird, I thought. And a smile came to my face.

CHAPTER SIX

THINGS GET UGLY

A breeze began to blow in from the west and the fog crept overhead. Seagulls squawked and seals barked on the rocks, practically demanding handouts from fishing boats. "What time did you say your flight was?" Brian asked, just after we'd finished lunch and began a stroll along the bay.

"Six," I replied, snapping a photo of an extra-chubby seal. "Our first team meeting starts at eight. Can't be late to that, the head coach is a stickler for time. She actually refused to let a couple of people try out for the World University Games because they missed an organizational meeting."

"Sounds like the military. Everyone's extra strict about time. You learn to adjust." Sometimes I forgot that Brian had been living a completely different kind of life during the past four years. The idea of being in the military was fascinating to me and I could have listened to him talk about his adventures

all day.

We walked on for a minute before he stopped and looked at me with a concerned expression on his face, "Now you've got me thinking about the clock. Are you sure you don't want to catch an earlier flight? I mean, I'm having a great time, but——"

"You're bored," I blurted out. Not the sort of thing Susan Ambler or Starling would have said. Why couldn't I learn to keep my big mouth shut?

"No, you could never bore me, Brit. Annoy, maybe, but bore?" We laughed and I took a picture of Brian. He tugged me along. "I was just thinking about the traffic. I mean, you're talking rush hour in Los Angeles, it could get pretty ugly."

"The meeting's at the team hotel. It's right by the airport," I assured him. "I'll be fine."

A musician was on the corner playing an electric guitar and Brian saw the opportunity to change the subject. "Just think, Brit," Brian teased, as I fumbled with another canister of film, "if your WNBA career doesn't work out, and the photography thing doesn't happen either, you could always come out here and set your grandmother's piano up by the cable car stop." I smiled at him and he we walked a few more steps, swerving into the street.

The wind blew and Brian brushed away a long strand of strawberry blonde hair that had blown across my face. "It's real good to see you Brit." He leaned in toward me and I felt the weight of the moment. Everything I'd thought about Brian and I had changed in the last hour. It turned out that he felt the same way about me that I felt about him back in high school. I *hadn't said anything because I was scared of what he would think, and he hadn't confessed to anything because he was scared of what Eric would think. Thoughts swirled through my head just before his lips touched mine. And then—HONK! A passing taxicab quickly alerted us that we were in the middle of the street. I pulled away, startled, and moved back onto the sidewalk following Brian's lead.*

It didn't take long for me to realize that I'd made the right decision in playing JV ball. I was a starter for the first time in my career and the team even elected Lisa and I as the captains. At first, the idea of leading the team frightened me, but after a few games, I realized that as the point guard, a leadership role was very natural. I was the coach on the floor. I would call the plays when we ran our half-court offense and was always aware of the game clock, the score, and what defense was being run against us. My teammates looked to me for direction and I was usually pretty good about keeping everyone on the same page. Out of everyone on the team, I played the most minutes that year and Coach Jensen said that when I was on the floor, her heart didn't beat quite as fast. I took that as a big compliment.

We had a freshman who was a phenomenal player, and this made my job much easier. Sandi Powers could "fill it up" from anywhere. So I made sure that if she had an inch, she had the ball. Unfortunately, like a lot of really good scorers, she was a ball hog. Once you passed to Sandi, you could forget about touching it until the next time it went down the court. As a captain (and a junior, two years older than Sandi), it was up to me to get her to change. I did it too, and by the second half of the season, she was a well-rounded player, scoring when she was open and delivering passes to teammates when she was covered.

Coach Jensen later told me that my greatest accomplishment that year was the way I led my team, particularly Sandi. She mentioned that this was something that never showed up on stat sheets and couldn't be taught, yet it was something every college coach looked for. College coach? Did she actually think I had a chance of playing in college? *Relax, you have to make the varsity first,* I thought.

I was feeling good about my game and had finally resigned myself to the reality that I wasn't going to be a superstar scorer. My strength and endurance were coming along and I was nearly perfect with my foul shots.

Everything was going great until we got to Madison. It was our second to last game and we were tied with five minutes left in the fourth. Lisa inbounded the ball to me and I brought it up-court, weaving through two defenders. I spotted Sandi under the basket and quickly fired a bounce pass in to her. She started to put it up, then realized I was open for three at the top of the key.

Her frantic pass flew over my head and I had to leap in order to grab it. When I landed on my feet, a Madison defender charged over and slapped the ball from my hands. We both dove for it, sliding along the slippery gym floor. Rolling toward the out-of-bounds line, we collided. An instant later the voice I heard screaming was my own. Unfortunately, when we tangled, her pointer finger (and expertly manicured nail) slashed into my right eyeball. I still shudder when I remember the scratchy, sharp pain.

Play was halted and both coaches took a look at me. My eye hurt so badly that I couldn't keep it open long enough to be examined. Eventually they determined that the injury wasn't too serious. Still, I was forced to sit out the rest of the game, which I'm happy to report we went on to win.

Mom made me see an eye specialist the next day just to make sure I was OK. I was, but Dr. Lopez insisted that I wear a special set of plastic glasses for the rest of the season. (Thanks a lot, doc.) They looked like swimming goggles and even I had to laugh at myself. Eric and Brian got a lot of mileage out of my "visual appliance."

Our JV record ended up being an impressive 14 and 5 and we went on to win the conference by a couple of games. Overall, it was a good season.

Although JV was over, varsity was still in full swing. They finished third in their section, making them eligible for the district tournament. But just before the tournament began, strange things started happening. First of all, Anita Ochoa quit the team without explanation, and in a fluke accident the next day, Roberta Johnson tore a ligament in her knee. Two roster spots had opened up the week the tournament began.

When Coach called me in and asked if I was ready to take on a new challenge, I was thrilled. Sandi moved up to varsity with me, filling the other slot to Lisa's chagrin. How I got there wasn't important. Gradually, I learned to cope with the fact that the rest of the team ignored my presence. If you were in our locker room, you would have thought Kendra and I had never met. It was a good thing Sandi moved up with me or I wouldn't have had anyone to sit with on the team bus.

None of that mattered, though. I was on the Jefferson girls' varsity. I didn't mind that my jersey number was thirteen and I didn't mind that everyone claimed the number had jinxed Roberta, causing her to tear a ligament. And it didn't even matter that Mom and Coach insisted I continue wearing my "visual appliance." I was finally where I wanted to be. Well, almost. I was still on the bench.

Spring grades came out the day of the district semifinals. I did pretty well, all A's and B's. I liked my classes and found that the discipline of basketball forced me to organize myself and use my time more wisely. Eric and Brian both made the honor roll too, which was important for them because these were the last set of grades sent out to colleges. Eric wasn't exactly sure what he wanted to do or where he wanted to go. He was good at math and science and was looking at Virginia College and Richmond Tech. Brian had his heart set on the Naval Academy and we all thought he had a pretty good shot at it.

But grades weren't such good news for one of my varsity teammates. Michelle Conners was failing English. I first heard the rumor during second period when Anne Zingerhoff, a Swedish exchange student, claimed that she overheard Stephanie Powell telling Nancy Davis that Michelle had failed her English midterm. I had to believe Anne because she never lied about that kind of stuff. So when I began to see the procession in and out of Coach Jensen's office around third period, I knew it must be true. As it turned out, she hadn't failed. But Michelle's English grade was a D: D for disaster, D for disqualified,

D for dismissed. Coach Jensen's rule was that if a player had any spring grades below a C, that player was benched until her grade came up or the teacher verified that she was making progress.

Coach gathered us all in the locker room for a team meeting the minute classes were over. She explained what had happened. Michelle was suspended and I would start in her place. I was nervous. I'm sure my facial expression made that clear. Coach smiled and patted me on the back, "Don't worry, we're behind you, Brit." Dirty looks from my teammates darted my way one by one (and sometimes two at a time). I was worried.

Thirty minutes after the bus arrived to take us to the game, I was going through warm-up drills in a daze. When the starting lineups were announced, my name was the very first one called. My first start on varsity would be in a critical road game. We were matched up against Shenandoah and the player of the year, Sherry Sterling. She was beautiful, smart, and as tough as they come.

I got over my butterflies as soon as the ball was tossed in the air for the opening tip-off. No time to worry now, I had to play my best. No, better than my best. Shenandoah got the tip and Sterling flashed down the court for a quick layup. *Defend the lane, Brit,* I cursed myself.

By the end of the first quarter, things were OK. I'd made a few mental errors, but we'd still played to a tie, eighteen-all. This was a fairly quick pace, definitely favoring Shenandoah's "run and gun" style. Coach told us in the huddle to slow things down and control the tempo. But no matter how much we tried, it seemed that every time Sherry Sterling touched the ball, she scored. Fortunately for us, Kendra was almost as hot as Sherry and we went into the locker room at the half trailing by only four.

Five minutes into the third quarter, we battled back to a tie. Things were going OK for me. I'd taken one shot from the floor, a fifteen footer that rimmed out. But I was holding my own with a steal here and there. But never, I admit, off of Sterling.

Then things got ugly. The avalanche began on a routine play. I was bringing the ball up-court after one of Sterling's nothing-but-net shots when she whizzed by me so fast I didn't even see her. The next thing I knew, I was running toward our basket without the ball. Sterling stole it from me in midair, taking it back down for a layup. I usually had a pretty good handle. In fact, during nineteen games on JV that year, the ball had only been stolen from me twice.

I took the inbound pass again and the instant I crossed the center stripe, Sherry did the same thing to me, scoring another basket. Six points in about thirty seconds. And to make things worse, on the very next play, the inbound pass went right through my fingers as if they were greased. Sterling grabbed the loose ball and made a jumper from the foul line, eight straight points. Mercifully, Coach Jensen called a time-out to calm me down. Everyone on our team shot the "evil eye" at me.

When we went back onto the court, I brought the ball up slowly and deliberately. We were down by ten. Kendra came out to meet me and I passed the ball safely to her. We dribbled around for what seemed like ten minutes, trying to get somebody, anybody, open. Kendra tossed it back to me. "Take it, Brit!" When I didn't immediately move, she shouted at me again. "Put it up!"

I obeyed and promptly launched an air ball that luckily bounced off Sterling's foot beneath the basket, spinning out of bounds. I wanted to disappear, vanish into thin air. But the ref retrieved the ball and handed it to Beth, who inbounded it to me again. Sterling saw that I was shaken and reached for another steal. Luckily, the ref called a foul this time.

I stepped up to the free-throw line, completely rattled. I took a deep breath. *At least I can redeem myself here,* I thought. I hadn't missed a foul shot since the first of December. I dribbled twice and stared at the rim, putting it up the way I always do. The ball hit the front of the rim——not even close. Kendra looked at me and shook her head. My hands started to shake as I went through my routine for the second shot. Concentrate, Brittany. Clank, off the side of the rim this time. And what was even worse was that Sterling grabbed the rebound and dribbled right by me on her way to a coast-to-coast layup.

Coach Jensen signaled for another time-out. When I got to the sidelines I had tears in my eyes, "You're a bundle of nerves, Brittany. Have a seat and calm down." I slunk off and sank down on the end of the bench. "Sandi!" Coach yelled briskly. "Take Kendra's position at forward. And Kendra, you bring the ball up. Come on, let's get back into this thing."

Sandi didn't have to be told twice. She came in and never looked back, firing up one shot after another. Some she made, some she missed, but she never stopped shooting. She scored thirteen points in the fourth quarter alone and we managed to hold on for a two-point victory. I didn't play another minute of that game.

With only one day of practice before the big game, everyone was tense and edgy. Kendra was constantly lobbying for Sandi to replace me in the lineup. But when Coach Jensen began practice, she started me at point guard again. It was a hard session, but a good one. Coach had everybody coming at me, trying to rattle me. That was just fine. I never wanted to be publicly humiliated the way I was at the Shenandoah game.

My teammates weren't any help in putting the experience behind me. I was sitting in the school cafeteria the day of the game, picking at my fruit salad, when Kendra and two other seniors sat down at the table. "About tonight," Kendra began, looking at the other girls and then at me, "we don't think you should play."

I looked up in total surprise.

Chris and Liz nodded. "You can tell Coach you're sick," Liz urged. "It happens all the time."

"Yeah," Chris chimed in, "you saw for yourself the other night. We're much better with Kendra at point guard and Sandi playing forward."

I knew they didn't have much confidence in me, but I had no idea they felt this strongly. My mouth must have hung open. I couldn't think of a thing to say.

"Just say that you don't feel well," Kendra said, standing, "or tell her you're scared. We don't really care what you say, as long as you don't play. You want the team to win, don't you?"

When I didn't answer they walked out, leaving me there alone. I have to say it was the worst I'd ever felt in my life. I looked up to see Brian standing over me. "I heard that," he said.

I swallowed hard, determined not to let him know how much what they said upset me.

"You're not going to let them frighten you off, are you?" His blue eyes had a hard, determined edge.

I stared off into space, biting my lip to keep from crying.

"I know you're stronger than that, Brit."

Brian was right. I stood up, stuck my chin out, and spoke with a newfound confidence, "You're right, I'm way stronger than that." I got up and gave Brian a hug, probably the first one we'd ever shared. Eventually I let go, but I have to admit, I could have stayed like that forever.

My last class of the day was world history and it ran a little late. I had to hustle. Racing to the locker room, I threw my gear into my red bag. When I got outside, most of the team had already boarded the bus. The rest of the players were waiting for Coach Jensen, who was in her office on the phone. Everyone ignored me and I ignored them, tossing my bag up with the others in the back of the bus. "I'm playing," I announced to no one in particular, finding a seat up front.

About five minutes later Coach came out of the gym and the rest of the team boarded the bus. It wasn't far to Middletown, the site of our game, but the traffic was bad so it took awhile. The bus was much quieter than usual. We were extra focused.

By the time we arrived, we all rushed off the bus, grabbed our gear, and headed for the locker rooms. It was going to be tight. The consolation game was already in the fourth quarter.

Somebody must have grabbed my bag by mistake, because it wasn't there when I got around to the back of the bus. When I finally made my way into the locker room, still searching for my bag, the rest of the team had already started changing. I glanced around, hoping to see it right away. Even though there were only a basic range of gym bags, most were fairly easy to identify. Some had stickers or patches on them. Some were torn, worn, big, small, bright, or faded. Mine was dark red and the zipper was broken——and it was definitely missing. Jackets and sweaters were tossed every which way in our haste to get changed, so I stalked around asking who'd seen my bag and trying to look under discarded clothing faster than it was piling up.

"Brittany, get a move on," Coach Jensen shouted.

I was starting to panic. Tears were beginning to form in my eyes. "I can't find my gym bag." I began to tear through the piles of clothes, my heart racing, blood thudding in my ears. I don't remember how long I was in the locker room alone after everyone else had dressed and was out. Eventually, I just slumped down on the cold, hard floor, unable to believe what was happening.

"Brittany?" Coach Jensen stormed into the locker room.

I nodded and was unable to keep the tears from coursing down my face. "I loaded it on myself. They didn't want me to play, they hid it."

She came over and knelt down beside me for a minute. Patting me on the shoulder, she whispered softly. "Let's hope there's another explanation, Brit." She shuffled through some loose clothes, "I'm so sorry this happened to you. When we find out who did this, they're in a lot of trouble. But the glasses, you know I can't let you out there without them, right?"

"I know," I managed to choke.

She stood up. "The game's about to start. Come on out and sit on the bench with us."

I managed to pull myself together, and after a while, I went out and sat on the end of the bench by the girl with the stat book. My eyes were so puffy I could hardly see out of them. Somehow I made it through without crying again.

When the game finally ended, I have to say I was relieved. We won in overtime, but I was too miserable to care. I overheard Eric tell Coach Jensen that he'd give me a ride home. I was thankful I didn't have to get back on the bus with the girls who'd been so anxious to keep me off the court that they'd done something with my bag.

I went to bed heartsick that night.

The next day, Mom gave us a ride to school. I begged her to let me stay home so I didn't have to face anyone, but as she said, "You have to go back sometime. The longer you stay away, the worse it'll be."

Actually, it wasn't too bad at all. Several of my classmates heard what had happened and were sympathetic. Coach Jensen called me in and asked me exactly what the girls had said to me at lunch.

Three days later, my missing gym bag was found in the back of a supply closet. When Coach questioned Kendra, Chris, and Liz, she found out everything she needed to know. They left her office suspended from the first game of the regional tournament.

I was eligible and I started. I don't think you'll be surprised to learn that we lost. South Roanoke was a great team and two of our starters were ineligible. Maybe we would have lost anyway, but we'll never know. Did the bag controversy make me even more unpopular with my teammates? With some, probably. But a few recognized that what happened wasn't my fault and blamed Kendra, Chris, and Liz for the whole thing.

CHAPTER SEVEN

SHERRY STERLING

"I think the parking garage is over there." I pointed toward an enormous hill and a blue neon sign that read PARK. Just as we started walking up the slope, a jet roared across the sky above us. Immediately, Brian jerked his head up.

I had to laugh. "You haven't changed a bit. Still distracted by anything that flies, huh?"

He grinned sheepishly, "That's not just something that flies, Brit, that's an F-16. Nothing more fun in the world than flying that thing."

I followed his gaze and we watched the silver jet streak past a tall, triangularly shaped building. "What's that?" I asked.

"An F-16 is a——"

"No, I mean the building."

"Oh, that's the Transamerica Pyramid. It's the tallest building in San Francisco. Great views from the top."

I glanced at my watch, then up at the building. "I think we have some time. If you feel like it."

Brian stopped in his tracks and grinned at me. "I thought you were afraid of heights." He reached out to touch a strand of my hair. "Whatever happened to the skinny little girl with freckles and braces?" There was a moment of silence and I'm sure I blushed. Brian grabbed my hand. "So, you want to go up?"

A moment later we were racing toward the entrance to the building. By the time we reached the lobby, a line had already formed. There were probably fifty people waiting for the elevator that led to the observation deck.

"You think you have time?" Brian asked, as we inched forward slowly.

I checked my watch again. "It's worth seeing, right?" I ventured.

"Best sight in the city," he acknowledged, "and the elevators are fast too."

"Then don't sweat it." I was really torn now. I needed to be at the airport in time to make my flight to Los Angeles. My watch read 3:39 and my flight was scheduled to depart at 6:00, which meant we'd board at about 5:30. I had less than two hours to see the top of this building, make it all the way down, get the rental car, navigate through traffic to the airport, get my bag, check in, and board the plane before takeoff. I was cutting things very close, but I just couldn't tear myself away from Brian.

"The Olympics are in Seattle this year, aren't they?" he asked.

"Yup, the Emerald City," I replied.

"If you make the team, I'll fly over the stadium with one of those banners with your name on it."

"Don't say that," I warned. "You'll jinx me."

"Still superstitious?" he teased, as we finally stepped onto the crowded elevator.

"I think I'm more superstitious than ever. You know I still have the Washington state quarter you gave me for good luck the first time I ever tried out for a team. I won't go anywhere without it. And wouldn't you know it, now I'm trying out for the Olympics——in Washington. Pretty weird, huh?" The minute these words were out of my mouth, I wished I could have taken them back. He probably didn't even remember giving me that quarter, so he definitely wasn't going to see the coincidence.

"You still have that quarter?" His voice rose and the dimple in his left cheek was deeper now and more wildly attractive than ever.

"I keep it in my shoe," I blushed slightly. "That's why I've been so lucky."

"I gave that to you when I coached the team you tried out with. I remember that." He continued, jokingly, "In fact, I was the one who suggested your position for you. Maybe I should be coaching the Olympic team."

The elevator stopped, reaching the top floor. We exited slowly and made our way to the observation deck. "What'd I tell you?" Brian said as we looked out across the bay. "Isn't this something?"

I looked down at the Golden Gate Bridge, Alcatraz,

and the fog rolling in, "It's beautiful," I was totally floored. "So what's better, this or the view from the cockpit?"

Brian smiled, "It's pretty close, but I'd have to give it to the cockpit." He put his arm casually around my shoulder, pointing toward an island in the middle of the bay. "That's Treasure Island, I spent a couple of months training there."

"Flying?" I managed to squawk, his nearness robbing me of my voice as well as my wits.

"No, I actually did flight school in Florida, then I trained on the F-16 in San Diego."

"You sure get around, Brian." Another brainless comment. Get a grip, Brittany.

He laughed and turned to look at me, his back to the windows. "Where's your camera? We can get someone to take a picture of the two of us. Maybe we can send it to Eric—tell him I'm giving you pointers on making the Olympic team."

I started to hand my camera over to him but was in such a daze that it slid right through my fingers and landed on the deck. Right away, the two of us knelt down to snatch it up. Our hands closed over the camera at the same time and my heart started to race inside my chest. I looked up to see Brian's eyes staring into mine. Then he reached out to me, his finger straying across the base of my chin. I closed my eyes as he leaned in to kiss me—right there on the observation deck, with both of us still kneeling on the ground to pick up the now-forgotten camera. I'd waited for that kiss for what seemed like forever.

Prom was a disaster. I got to go during my junior year,

which was kind of a tradition in my high school, with all the senior guys taking a junior girl. You can imagine my pain when I found out that Brian had asked Sherry Sterling. Eric, whom you would think might have known better, filled me in on every detail from the corsage to the color of Sherry's dress. (For a smart guy, my brother can be really dense sometimes.) But I guess if he had no idea how desperately I loved Brian, then Brian probably didn't either. So at least I still had my pride.

Marc Iaccone was my date. He was tall, like six-foot-five or something, and had this weird habit of saying everything twice. When he came up to me at my locker and said, "Hey Brit, we're sharing a limo with Brian and Eric, we're sharing a limo with Brian and Eric," I knew I was in trouble. Picture this: an hour-long limousine ride with me wedged in between Susan Ambler and Sherry Sterling. It was a nightmare.

I don't think I said a word the entire ride. I tried to avoid making eye contact with Brian, Susan, Sherry, and especially my date, Marc. Every time I looked his way I thought he was going to try and kiss me. And that was the last thing I wanted! "This limo's huge, this limo's huge," Marc whispered to me just as we arrived.

Not huge enough, I thought, inching away from him.

Six months later, with the prom disaster in the rearview mirror, I was a senior at Jefferson and on top of the world. Eric had settled on Richmond Tech and Brian went off to the Naval Academy, taking my heart with him. (Although I don't suppose he ever realized it.) That winter, I approached varsity basketball tryouts with more confidence, having returned to the camp at Tennessee College again that summer. When I got back home, I knew something had clicked for me on the basketball court. I was twice the player I had been a year earlier. Plus, I'd grown a lot from the painful experience of having my teammates hide my gym bag.

Despite the bag controversy, Kendra turned out to be OK. She must have apologized a thousand times and even bought me a new bag, as a gesture of friendship. That entire fall, she, Lisa, and I practiced relentlessly. So we weren't surprised when we all made the team and the starting lineup, along with Sandi and Beth Silver.

For the three of us, it was our last year at Jefferson and we were determined to make the most of it. I was still the playmaking point guard and had developed a good jump shot to go along with my passing and game management skills. Plus, I hardly ever turned the ball over. My stat line usually looked something like this: eight points, ten assists, three or four steals, a few rebounds, and no turnovers.

By mid-season, we were undefeated. College scouts appeared at our games and Kendra began getting so many letters from them, her postman told her he was going to ask for combat pay. She got attention from colleges we'd never even heard of. I was a little jealous, but I was also realistic. Not many schools waste precious scholarships on a player whose claim to fame is four steals per game and a 91 percent free-throw average.

Nothing about my game set me apart from the multitalented players across the country. When I would approach scouts after games, they would point out reasons they were passing me over. They told me that I couldn't shoot accurately off the dribble and that I had a tough time rebounding because of my height. And even though I was complimented several times on being a good defender, they told me repeatedly that they were concerned I wouldn't be able to defend bigger guards (which was most of the girls playing Division 1 basketball).

"The thing is," one scout told me, "you've got a big heart in a real small body. Any team that offered you a scholarship would be going out on a limb." Although comments like these discouraged me, I didn't give up. I wrote letters and sent tapes to every major basketball program in the country. Unfortunately, I never got one response. But that wasn't going to stop me from trying to walk onto a basketball team somewhere.

The college bug had bitten us all. By December of my senior year, it seemed like that was all we could talk about. The question of the day was always, "So, where are you going in the fall?" For Kendra, it seemed obvious. Connecticut College, one of the top basketball programs in the country, had recruited her. She signed a letter of intent to attend school and play basketball for the eastern powerhouse on the first day of commitments. We all learned the Connecticut fight song and barked like dogs (hey, they're the Pit Bulls) every time Kendra took the floor at practice. After she licked the stamp and mailed the letter, she was "relieved to have all the fuss over with."

I was amazed by this comment. With no one paying any attention to me, I wished that I could experience some fuss, even just a little bit of fuss. But nobody was fussing much about a five-foot-three-inch point guard who averaged eight points a game. Despite the overwhelming reality that I probably wouldn't be able to play college basketball, there was some good news. My

SAT scores were great, even better than Eric's had been. (Naturally, I didn't waste any time calling to let him know.) Plus, I had gotten excellent grades in school, so getting into a good college wasn't going to be a problem for me. I was looking to attend a small school, one with a good fine arts program and a basketball team that I could try to walk on. But my senior season was going to be a huge factor in determining my future as a basketball player.

Luckily, that season was by far our most successful. We clicked. There is no other way to say it. Every time we stepped onto the floor we were a unit, playing the game together like a band playing a piece of music perfectly. So we weren't too surprised when we won the conference and earned a bye in the first round of the section tournament. This meant that we automatically advanced to the second round.

Our game was on a Wednesday night, but on Tuesday, we sat in the stands and watched Shenandoah blow East Fairfax out of the gym. Once again, I would have to go through Sherry Sterling to reach the section finals. Sterling scored twenty-six points that night, and for the year, was just behind Kendra as the number two scoring leader in the conference.

My feud with Sherry was heightened after a phone conversation with my brother at Richmond Tech. I told him that we would be playing against Shenendoah's Sherry Sterling, and he said that Brian told him that Sherry had been up to Annapolis for a football game. I supposed this meant that she was dating Brian. This made me crazy. On the court, she'd always had my number, and now she was getting to me off the court as well. When we took the floor that Wednesday night, I couldn't wait for my chance to beat her.

81

Both teams came out excited, but we played completely out of control early on. By the end of the first quarter, Lisa and I had two fouls each. The game was tied at sixteen and the big shooters on both teams were hot. I had two points on a jump shot that I took right over the top of Sterling. (I have to say it felt extra good to score on her.) But I knew my responsibility was to get the ball to Kendra and Sandi in good positions for them to score. If I started getting into a shooting contest with Sterling, we would lose the game for sure. So I maintained my focus, passing into the post whenever I saw the opportunity. Now that I had hit a jumper, though, Sterling had to come out further to defend me. This opened some good passing lanes inside, helping me to seven assists in that first quarter alone.

We trudged into the locker room at halftime, clinging to a two-point lead. Everyone was huffing and puffing and not really speaking to one another. Coach Jenson sensed our physical and emotional fatigue right away. She started clapping her hands and turned the faucets on at the sinks. She then told each of us to place our heads under the faucet for a few seconds. Not only was this refreshing, but funny as well. We all began laughing when the cold water hit our heads and the mood lightened.

When we came out for the third quarter, we were calmer, but still very much aware of protecting our two-point lead. Sandi inbounded the ball and I brought it up-court, passing over to Kendra, as she split the defenders in the lane. She drove right to the basket and laid it in exactly as we'd drawn it up in the locker room. Up by four.

On Shenendoah's next possession, my fingers were itching for a steal. Sterling dribbled by me and I reached out, managing to tip the ball as she passed. Sandi grabbed it and raced back to our goal for an easy layup. Sterling shot a fiery look my way and I glanced quickly at the scoreboard——we were up 46 to 40. Coach Jensen held up her hand in a clenched fist, which meant a full-court press. Coach Jensen was hoping to build on our lead by using defense to create turnovers.

I pestered Andee Kim, the Shenandoah guard trying to inbound the ball. I jumped, flailed my arms and was just a complete nuisance. Andee couldn't get the ball past half-court and was forced to call a time-out.

"Good," I shouted to nobody in particular, clapping my hands and looking at Sterling. "Let's use up those timeouts!" My outburst surprised even me. I was usually pretty quiet on the court. But when I looked at Sherry, all I could think about was her and Brian watching that football game together. It made me want to scream.

On the inbounds pass, they caught us flat-footed. We were so excited about our lead, we lost some of our intensity and opened the window for a comeback. Sterling quickly climbed right through. She put the ball up from the corner and Sandi fouled her in the process. Naturally, sure-shot Sterling made it a three-point play and, now, a three-point game. But this was a war for me, and it was very personal. Right away I came back down and hit a three-pointer over her outstretched hand with seven seconds left in the quarter, increasing our lead back to six. I stared over at Sterling again, but sure enough, on the next play she answered me right back. As the buzzer sounded, she threw up a prayer from half-court. Somehow, it slammed off the backboard and into the hoop. So by the end of the third quarter, we led 50 to –47 in a tight contest.

The fourth quarter started out more like a wrestling match than a basketball game. It was brutal. Each trip down the floor, Shenendoah would pound the ball inside. After they'd established their interior scoring, they began zeroing in on Sandi. They knew she was our youngest starter, and they thought they could rattle her. They were right. During the next four minutes, whomever Sandi was guarding defensively got the ball for Shenendoah. And on the offensive end, every time Sandi touched the ball, they'd scream, "Shoot! Shoot!" They put the entire game on her shoulders and she folded like a newspaper. We all knew Sandi liked to shoot, but we quickly found out that she didn't like to be heckled. The pressure caused her to completely lose concentration. She threw the ball away three times up the floor in a row and was near tears.

Coach was forced to pull her from the game just to calm her. Now clinging to a one-point lead, Shenandoah brought it back up the floor. I got great position in front of Sterling and she finally got called for charging. Her jet black eyes flashed at me in anger. She said something under her breath that I didn't quite catch, but I knew she wasn't wishing me good luck. I stared into her eyes and it was as if she and I were the only ones on the floor. It was like an old western showdown, except instead of shooting bullets, we shot basketballs.

There was a pause in the action and I looked over at the crowd for a minute, noticing a man sitting with about ten small children around him. Some of them were holding up signs with Sherry's name on it, and they all looked just like her, so I assumed this was her family. I wondered how such a nice family could belong to Sherry. It just didn't seem to fit. Her dad looked busy, wiping ice cream from his son's face with two little kids sitting on his lap while he held another in his arms. *Where's her mother,* I thought. But this fleeting question quickly exited my head as the ref's whistle blew again and Beth Silver inbounded the ball to me.

I dribbled down the court and tossed up a shot right away. I missed it, but Sterling had caught me on the elbow, a foul. I went to the free-throw line and made the first one with ease. Then I took a deep breath and put the other one up. It ricocheted around the rim forever, but finally dropped. I sighed with relief. We now led by one with two minutes to play.

Andee Kim took the ball for Shenandoah and dribbled past Kendra as Lisa and I closed in at the top of the lane to cut off the path to Sterling.

That's when I felt it first, a sharp tug on my hair, so sudden and so strong, it snapped my neck back. I jerked my head around and thought I saw Sterling's hand leave my hair as she gathered in the ball. She put it up and in before I could make another move. I complained to the ref but he ignored my plea.

Shenandoah went ahead by one.

I inbounded the ball to Sandi over the heads of two Shenandoah players. When she caught it, she passed it to Kendra who was covered. Sandi didn't want anything to do with the ball. Kendra bounced it back out to me and I put it up from the top of the key. I knew that it was in right when I released it. Swish! I looked over at Sterling again.

Thirty seconds left. Now we led by one again, 66 to 65. At this point, I had scored eighteen points, tying my season high. Andee dribbled past half-court, looking frantically for Sterling to get open. The next thing we knew, Sterling was on the ground, screaming. The whistle sounded and the referee pointed to Lisa. She heaved a huge sigh, starting to say something to the official, and then snapping her mouth shut and running to the bench. Lisa had fouled out, putting Sterling on the line for two shots with six seconds to go.

She sank the first one, tying the game, then clutched the ball dramatically. She eyed the basket and put it up. This one was off target and we all rushed into the paint. It bounced off the rim back toward the line. A dozen or more grabbing, scratching, clawing hands fought to catch it.

Somewhere near the center of the pack of sweaty, slick bodies, I felt the ball come to me. Just as my fingers closed on it, something hit me in the stomach so hard that I saw stars. A second later, I heard a tremendous roar and then the buzzer.

When I looked up from the bottom of the pile, the game was over.

Sterling had charged the pile with legs and arms flailing. She practically vaulted over everyone to score the winning basket. We lost by two points. Our season was over, and for the seniors, our careers at Jefferson were too.

After the game I thought a lot about college next year. I wondered if I would be able to walk onto a team. I thought about getting another shot at Sterling. But more than anything, I thought about the possibility that I had just played the last game of my basketball career.

CHAPTER EIGHT

NORTHERN VIRGINIA

After about twenty minutes on the observation deck, Brian and I were ready to head back down and make our way to the airport. But a security guard approached us just as we reached the elevator doors, "I don't know if you folks felt it, but we just had a slight earthquake. Nothing to worry about, but the elevators are all shut down for an hour or so. When Mother Nature gives us a wake-up call like that, our power grid shuts down immediately. Just a precaution." The look on my face was one of disbelief. I was going to miss my flight. The man continued, "If you're in a hurry the staircase is to your left." There was only one choice——forty-three flights of stairs.

After running down to about the twentieth floor, Brian and I were both completely out of breath. He coughed a few times, "We better start walking or we're not going to make it."

Our pace slowed to a quick walk, *"What time is it, Brian?"* I panted, as we continued trooping down what seemed like endless flights of stairs.

"You're not wearing a watch?" he laughed. *"I thought you were the one with the plane to catch."*

"For your information, admiral, I am wearing a watch," I huffed, *"but I need to conserve my energy."*

"Too tired to lift up your arm?" he teased. *"How are you going to make the Olympic Team?"*

Now this was the Brian I remembered from my childhood, always giving me a hard time. *"Just answer the question."* I forced a smile, but was actually beginning to get quite nervous.

"Four fifteen." Brian confessed. *"Hey, at least we're climbing down now and not up."* He was much calmer than I was. But then again, he didn't have a 6:00 plane to catch.

Out of breath and nearly out of time, we stumbled onto the city streets from the stairwell. When we reached the corner of Columbus we were in for another surprise. *"Uh oh,"* Brian moaned. *"Looks like the traffic lights are out too."* And that wasn't even the worst of it. The city streets were in a gridlock. Horns were honking, lights were flashing, and my heart was pounding through my chest. All my work, all my dreams; everything was vanishing right in front of me. How could I be so stupid?

"I'm getting really worried, Brian," I groaned with tears starting to well up in my eyes.

"We'll make it," he said, rubbing his hand on my back as we turned into the parking garage.

"No more stairs," I gasped.

"We're only parked on the third level. Want a piggy-back?"

I playfully slugged him in the arm, "If it's more than three flights, I might take you up on it."

About nine months after that section game against Shenandoah, I walked onto the Northern Virginia campus as an eighteen-year-old college freshman. I wouldn't say that deciding what school to attend was an extremely tough decision for me. After just one visit in the spring of my senior year of high school, I was sold on UNV. And after just a few weeks here, I knew I'd made the right choice. By October I'd decided that my classes were great and I'd already made a bunch of close friends, despite spending most of my spare time honing my shots for basketball tryouts.

It was a dismal, rainy fall afternoon when we finally gathered in the gym for the tryout. Although everybody figured that Coach Fleming was looking to find two more guards, some girls who were more natural forwards ended up trying out, too. That made me a little nervous, since forwards often tend to be bigger guns. There were seventeen of us competing for just two positions. The other twelve spots on the team were filled with scholarship players. I knew I had to play my very best, especially since all seventeen of the girls I was competing against had been good players on their high school teams. And as per usual on the basketball court, I was the smallest one there.

What was even worse, though, was that today was the

only day of tryouts. I was sure that Coach Fleming was going to take one look at me and wonder why I even bothered to come out. Each time I passed him I walked on my tiptoes and took a deep breath to make myself look bigger. I don't think I was fooling anyone.

Based on some short conversations in the locker room, I found out that sixteen of us were freshmen. Only one, Rosa Santos, was a sophomore. I could see right away that she would be the toughest to beat out. She'd transferred from a junior college in Los Angeles, and she already had a year of college basketball under her belt. Rosa was tough and scrappy with a great three-point shot.

Right after we'd changed and were out on the floor, Coach Fleming matched us up for some three-on-three games. We played for ten minutes and then rotated out. We did this for three straight hours! At the beginning of the day I actually thought I had a chance. Rosa would make the team, no question. And it looked to me like the other vacancy would go to the player who stood out the most from the other girls in the next three hours. Now I don't normally take a lot of shots, but today, I was prepared to do whatever was necessary.

I played well and was sure that Coach Fleming would at least have to consider me. Up until the end, I was sure that I was right on the bubble. This meant that Coach Fleming's decision concerning me could go either way. But in the last game I played, pitted against Rosa, I put on a show that I hoped would make me the standout for that second spot.

By the time the game had ended, I'd managed three steals, a blocked shot and four defensive rebounds. That's right,

I got four rebounds! But on the offensive side, I was nothing short of spectacular. In less than ten minutes, I had scored all eleven of our points and hadn't missed a shot.

"OK, girls," Coach Fleming yelled, blowing his whistle. "That's it."

We trooped off the court and collapsed on the benches. He ambled over and tossed a ball to Rosa. "You all put up a good fight. So thanks for coming out." This was a much different tryout than any other I had been to. Mainly because nobody that was there (with the exception of Rosa) expected to make the team. After all, most of the roster was made up of scholarship players and fifteen out of the seventeen girls who tried out would be cut. Coach Fleming knew this and was quick and matter-of-fact when he said, "Rosa Santos and little Brittany Bristol, I'll see you two tomorrow afternoon for practice."

Little Brittany Bristol was on a college basketball team! How about that? I made sure to call pretty much everyone I knew that night and tell the news. Overall, I think people were pretty shocked. Everyone in my life had been rooting for me, but I don't think anyone (besides Mom and Dad) truly believed I was going to do it. The surprise I heard in their voices added to my feeling of accomplishment. By making the team I'd done something no one, including myself, expected me to do.

When I told old Mrs. Ripley, my piano teacher, she nearly made me cry. "People told you that mountain was too high to climb. But your heart was bigger than your head and you tried anyway. Now how's it feel to be standing on the top?" It felt great.

When the season opened a month later, Clarissa Jack-

son, our highly coveted power forward, was the only freshman starting. I was just happy to be there. I knew that as a freshman walk-
on, my playing time would be limited. We had three seniors filling
the two guard spots already and the other forward position as well.
I was the third string point guard, so I kept a pretty low profile, just
trying to learn the system and navigate my way through the treach-
eries of the locker room. And let me tell you, in our locker room
that year, it was extremely treacherous.

I don't know what the team chemistry was like before I
came, but given the girls on it, I doubt it was great. I guess the
trouble started because of the situation with Clarissa. She took
the place of a popular senior who'd started at power forward
for the past two seasons. Needless to say, the other seniors were
angry at what they thought was an injustice. They pointed this
anger directly at Clarissa. And that was only the beginning of
the trouble.

The upperclassmen refused to pass the ball to Clarissa
and although Coach Fleming pleaded with them, nothing he
said in practice or during the games seemed to make any difference. He had lost total control of his team. To be honest,
Clarissa didn't make things any easier on herself.

"I'm headed to the dining hall," I said, as I picked up
my gym bag after practice one afternoon. I looked over at
Clarissa. "Do you want to come?"

"I'm busy," she mumbled, snatching up her bag and
storming out the door of the locker room.

"Miss Personality," mocked Roz Smythe, the senior
who'd lost her starting position to Clarissa.

"You got that right," twittered Amy Ross and Reina

Klein, the other starting seniors.

All the senior girls were very close, since three started and the other two were our top subs. But their heads were in another place altogether. They certainly didn't seem to care much about basketball. Rosa was convinced it was because the team had never been very good and they simply had no pride.

But the senior clique was only one problem. Kelly Washington, our junior center, was tight with the other two juniors on the team who, oddly, were both centers also. They went everywhere together and rarely spoke to the rest of us. So there was yet another exclusive clique. Plus, the two sophomores, Kayla O'Grady and Aziz Khan, that Rosa joined when she replaced the player who didn't make grades, held it against Rosa personally. This was because Rosa replaced Kayla's twin sister, Karla.

Then there were us freshmen. We weren't really a clique, we were kind of just there. Besides Clarissa and me, there was Ming Kuo, a Chinese girl from New York City who spoke very little English, and Andrea Summers, a pretty girl from a small town in North Carolina. I was convinced the only reason Andrea played basketball was to be seen. She had a wicked jumper, but her "pretty-girl" posturing made me question how she'd hold up in a game.

So, given this cast of characters, it was not surprising that by the time we came back to school after winter break, our team was dead last in the conference. Nobody, I mean nobody, came to our games. Morale was very low. And Clarissa, who was one of the top high school basketball players in America last year, was averaging less than eight points per game. I could tell she was really down about it too, even though she never said anything. And if the media had ever actually been to one of our games, they would have seen why she wasn't scoring. You can't score if no one ever passes you the ball!

One evening in late January, I misplaced my history notebook and remembered I'd last seen it in the locker room. I hurried back across campus. It was dusk and just beginning to snow. Hamilton Gym was almost dark, but a few lights were still on. I let myself in and just as I touched the door to the locker room, I could hear someone sobbing softly. Now, I didn't want to intrude, but I had a history test the next morning. I had to go in and get my notebook.

I eased the door open and stepped in quietly. Right away I saw my notebook on the bench near the shower area. I knew someone was in there, but I didn't see a soul. I tiptoed across, and just as my hand landed on the face of my notebook, I saw Clarissa. She was sitting on a bench, hunched over, hugging her knees and crying.

"Clarissa? What's wrong?" I could hardly go away and pretend I didn't see her. She looked up at me, tears streaming down her face. "What is it?" I said. "Are you hurt?"

She shook her head. "Just go away," she hissed, her voice hard and angry.

Well, like Eric used to say, I'm persistent. So I sat down beside her, silent at first, but then I reached over and touched her shoulder, "What is it?"

She started to jerk away but then collapsed into herself and started wailing. "I hate it here!" she sobbed. "I want to go home."

"Everybody feels like that sometimes." I rubbed her shoulder. "Did something happen?"

"No," she spat out through tears and sniffles, "just the same old thing. Everybody hates me, nobody likes me."

"Nobody hates you," I insisted. "Nobody really knows you."

"They all want me out of here," she continued.

"How can you say that?" I reasoned. "You're a great player. Any team in the country would want you."

"Any team but this one. They don't even let me touch the stupid ball."

I sighed. How could I argue with that? "They're just jealous."

"Teammates aren't supposed to be jealous," she choked out.

"You're right. But this team isn't like any I've ever played on." I thought for a while. "How about you?"

She shook her head.

"Well, maybe we can turn it around," I suggested, although I didn't have the slightest idea how.

Clarissa raised her head and looked at me, her large brown eyes watery. "You and me?"

What was I getting us into? "We could try," I replied, with more conviction than I felt.

Clarissa fumbled in her pocket for a tissue. "Problem with me is," she said, "it's hard for me to get to know people."

"You're just shy," I said.

"You got it, Brittany. That's me, 'Miss Personality' herself," she snorted. "I hear what they call me."

"Don't let them bother you," I scolded. "You know, it isn't any easier that you're a freshman and part of the starting lineup—"

"And I replaced a really popular senior," she finished my sentence.

I agreed, smiling. "Next year, five seniors are graduating. Everything will change then. You just have to stick it out."

"But what can we do about it right now?" she asked.

"I don't know," I said, honestly. "Maybe take them out to dinner."

Clarissa began to brighten up. "What if we made cookies and invited the girls over to our floor—"

I started to like this idea, "—on like a Sunday night, when we don't have practice," I chimed in.

"—and maybe we can get to know each other—"

"—and talk." I thought a minute. This wasn't such a bad idea.

The following Sunday afternoon, Clarissa and I sat in the kitchen on our floor, studying for an English exam while chocolate chip cookies baked in the oven. I'm a total loss in the kitchen, but Clarissa really knew how to cook. She said her grandmother taught her.

We invited Ming and Andrea to help us. Andrea had a date, but Ming came, all eyes and ears. By the time the cookies were out of the oven, though, Andrea appeared after canceling her date. We'd invited the rest of the team over, too, but only Rosa came.

Our season ended in late February and we'd managed to move up a spot to the second last place in the conference. In the month since we'd begun the Sunday night get-togethers, those of us who came grew closer. We freshmen were always there, even if it meant Andrea had to stand up a date. We could count on Rosa's presence, and sometimes one or two of the juniors came too.

At the end of the season, Coach Fleming announced his resignation and we were all buzzing about who might be named to replace him. With five graduating seniors and two sophomores transferring out to other colleges, our team figured to have a whole new look next year. For us freshman, it couldn't have been more exciting. Next season, as sophomores, we would each be a critical part of the team.

CHAPTER NINE

SOPHOMORE YEAR

We finally made it to the car on the third floor of the parking garage. When Brian turned the engine on, my eyes went immediately to the digital clock on the dashboard. "Four twenty-four."

We zipped down the ramps and headed for the exit. Just as we turned the corner to exit the garage Brian slammed his fist against the steering wheel. There was a line of cars in front of us at the cashier's booth. What was worse was that it appeared that the gate was stuck closed, and with the electricity out, there was no way to open it. We were stuck. Horns were honking all around us and Brian jumped out of the car, approaching the booth.

A tall man with a grizzly beard spoke helplessly as Brian approached him, "Power's out and the bar won't go up."

"You've got to be kidding," Brian said.

"I wish I was, but there's nothing I can do." The man shrugged his shoulders and took a sip from a can of soda. I put my head in my hands, frustrated that I was going to be cut from the team before I'd even been given a chance. Sherry Sterling was probably having dinner with the coaching staff right now and I was stuck behind six cars in a parking garage.

All around us, people were starting to panic along with me. The cashier came out of the booth and surveyed the gate bar that was stuck in the down position. Brian spoke over his shoulder and the man nodded his head again and again. Finally I heard the man say, "You can try."

Brian stood in front of the gate and shouted to the line of cars, "Does anyone have a screwdriver?"

Immediately, one guy popped open his trunk and started rummaging around. "I got one." He held up a miniscrewdriver and tossed it to Brian.

A second later, Brian was bending over the bar and I jumped out to help him. He began unscrewing the bar from its moorings. I got down on my knees and took over unscrewing the bolts as soon as Brian had loosened them. In only a few minutes, Brian was able to lift the heavy bar aside. He stood and shouted to the crowd, "OK, pay up and get out."

The crowd cheered as Brian took a quick bow and we rushed back to the car.

"See, Brit," he said, as he turned the ignition, "we make a great team."

"I've got to hand it to you," I began, "That was great." I smiled. There was still a chance I could make my flight.

I spent the summer before my sophomore year working as a counselor at a basketball day camp back home in Oak Grove. This was a good job because I got to play basketball every single day. Eric was home for the summer too, working at a local vet's office. I saw him all the time and we even played a couple of one-on-one games in the backyard. I'm happy to say that I won them all. We didn't see Brian though, because he was on a summer cruise with the Navy.

With high school in the rearview mirror and my promise to Mom as well, dust gathered on Gran's piano. I neither touched it nor mentioned it. Neither did Mom, but I did catch her looking sadly at it a couple of times. Those few months went by in a flash and before I knew it I was back at school.

Sophomore year at UNV got off to a great start. Our new coach, Dana Hollins, came from the East Parksville University staff in southern Virginia, and she brought in a couple of junior college transfers, both of whom won starting spots, one at point guard, and the other at forward. Kelly, our returning center, was now a senior. Clarissa continued to play at power forward and Rosa won the other starting guard spot. I moved up a slot to the backup point guard position and Coach Hollins offered me a full scholarship for the next three years at UNV. Mom and Dad were thrilled.

We continued our Sunday evening cookie parties. With five freshmen and two juniors new to the team, everyone began showing up the same way they did for practice. The team really began to gel together. We were still different personalities, but we were learning a lot about one another.

Clarissa was more at ease now too, and after eating about

a thousand of her chocolate chip cookies, I was beginning to think that she might be a better cook than a basketball player. Ming blossomed in the informal atmosphere of the dorm kitchen get-togethers, and we were introduced to a wonderful array of exotic Chinese desserts. By the second half of sophomore year, she was speaking English like she'd been born here. And Andrea had traded in boys for basketball. (Well, some boys.)

Although I didn't get a ton of playing time my sophomore year, I still considered it a successful season. I would sub in for about six minutes a game, usually at the end of the first half and the beginning of the second. Even though I wasn't starting, just being out there in pressure situations was great experience for me. As a team, we improved over last season. Clarissa was our leading scorer—in double figures every game—and she led the conference in rebounding too.

Our strong regular season earned us a trip to the NCAA tournament. That was the good news. The better news was that we found ourselves advancing past the first round. Up until this year, UNV had only been invited to the tournament five times, the last one being nearly ten years ago, so making it past the first round was a special honor. But our excitement quickly faded when we looked across the court at our second round opponents, Southern Maryland. They were big, athletic, and mean looking. The Crabs were ranked seventh in the nation, and were the highest-ranked team we'd faced all year long. Winning this game would be a small miracle.

As it turned out, we played the best game of our season that day. Still, with three minutes left, Southern Maryland was ahead by two points. We'd managed to match them basket for basket until Pip McMann, the junior transfer and our starting point guard, fouled out with eight minutes left.

"Brittany!" Coach Hollins screamed. "Eight minutes left, this is your team now." When Coach uttered those words, a chill ran down my spine. I checked into the game with more excitement than ever before. This game was nationally televised and I was going to be playing the rest of the half.

I brought the ball up-court deliberately, determined to control the pace. Right away Dixie Cruz, the top Crab, lunged for a steal. I slung the ball behind my back to Rosa, who put it in the air from well beyond the three-point arc. Three! We now led by one. The excitement in the arena was starting to build.

But Southern Maryland answered us immediately with a jump shot from the corner. I began dribbling up-court again, this time, looking for Kelly inside. She wove her way under the basket and back out, undetected by Southern's defense. I glanced in Rosa's direction and then faked a pass to Clarissa. Once Cruz bit, I quickly arched the ball over to Kelly, who'd come back under the basket. She tapped it in and a whistle sounded. Foul on Southern!

Kelly came to the line with us leading, 56 to 55. She fired. Bottom! 57 to 55. A two-point lead with less than two minutes to play. I was controlling the game and distributing the ball to my teammates in positions for them to score. This was the definition of a point guard.

On the ensuing play, I managed to get my hand on the inbounds pass and tip the ball. Rosa dove to the floor, grabbing the ball and passing it to me. I raced the few yards to the basket for an easy lay up, my first two points of the tournament.

"Yes, Brit!" Clarissa shouted. "Up by four!"

We went to a full-court press, but Southern avoided us easily. Cruz caught a pass near the baseline, dribbled back out and put up a three-point shot. Swish! A collective, "Oh" from the crowd signaled that everyone was rooting for the underdog tonight. I heard the announcer calling the game as I dribbled past him at half-court. "What a big shot from Cruz and Southern Maryland is right back in the game!"

Clinging to a one-point lead, I bounced the ball over to Clarissa with just over a minute left. Heather Jackson was in her face immediately, swinging her arms wildly for a steal. There was a flurry of hands and just before a whistle sounded, I heard Clarissa scream, holding her hand over her right eye.

In one of the worst calls I'd ever seen, the referee whistled for a jump ball. Clarissa had been jabbed in the eye after being slapped in the head two or three times and he was calling a jump ball? I kept my mouth shut and bumped knuckles with Ming, who came onto the floor to replace Clarissa.

To our dismay, the possession arrow was theirs. Southern brought the ball up and we stiffened our backs, anxious to protect our one-point lead. They moved the ball around the perimeter for a while. Finally, with forty seconds left in the game and only five left on the shot clock, their taller guard, Sue Whitt, flipped the ball to Cruz, who put it up right away. Another three-pointer. Swish!

And just like that, we were down by two. I wasn't going to give up though. I dribbled up-court through heavy pressure from their guards. The announcer's voice was in my ear again, "Little Brittany Bristol," (this had become my nickname) "the sophomore walk-on, is hounded near half-court. She weaves through the defense pretty easily. She's done an excellent job since replacing Pip McCann." *Thanks,* I thought. But when I crossed the half-court line, his voice faded and I passed over to Rosa, who quickly threw it in to Ming. She was fouled immediately and went to the line, making both shots and pulling us back into a tie at 61 to 61.

"Watch Cruz!" I yelled, as Ming ran by me. I dogged Whitt, hoping to get my hand on the ball, but again she tossed it to Cruz as soon as they were across the line and Cruz lit it up with yet another three-pointer, this time with my hand right in her face. She was on fire!

After we brought the ball up, Southern fouled Rosa. Even though she made both shots, we were still down one. There were twelve seconds left when Whitt brought the ball up-court. I got position just outside the half-court line, forcing Whitt to go around me, while Rosa stuck to Cruz like glue. From nowhere, Ming joined me on the double team and slapped the ball away from Whitt. Everyone dove to the floor to retrieve the ball. Somehow, I grabbed it and started dribbling toward their basket. There was nobody between me and an easy lay up. But I'd been so focused on getting that loose ball that I forgot about the clock. The buzzer sounded before I reached half-court. Southern Maryland advanced and we went home.

What followed was a long, hot summer.

CHAPTER TEN

INCH BY INCH

A chilly wind began to blow in from the bay as Brian struggled to maneuver through the traffic-clogged streets. Nervously, I began to flick off my red nail polish with the silver stars.

Brian looked over at me, "Come on," he laughed, "try to think about something else." He pulled the car around a couple of trucks and made a right turn. "The streets will be less crowded once we get away from the financial district."

I tried to take my mind off the flashing digital clock on the dashboard. "So," I said, taking a deep breath and making a conscious effort not to look anywhere near the stupid thing, "how long will you be in Bremerton?"

"Until Uncle Sam decides he wants me to go somewhere else," Brian shrugged.

"Well, are you happy?" I had no idea why I was asking

such a serious question. This race-against-the-clock thing must have really been stressing me out.

"Couldn't be happier," he grinned. "I'm seeing the world. What about you, Brit?"

"Oh, just taking in the great American traffic jam." I muttered sarcastically.

This comment made Brian laugh again. "When will you know about the trials?" He asked, trying to distract me.

"You mean if I even make it to trials?"

"You'll make it, Brit, if I have to grab an F-16 and fly you there myself, OK?"

I had to smile. "I should know by the end of the week." I swallowed the remainder of this reply, the one I'd been telling everyone else in my life. This response usually began with me graciously talking about how nice it was to even be asked to try out, and how I couldn't possibly hope for anything more than the experience of competing. In actuality, this wasn't the truth. "I'd give anything to make the Olympic team," I confided in Brian, surprising even myself. I continued, "I mean, representing America would be the chance of a lifetime. Plus, if I make it, a WNBA team is sure to sign me up. Playing basketball as my job," I smiled. "Now that would be something."

"Do you know anybody else going to the WNBA?" Brian asked.

"Yeah, my best friend Clarissa." I paused, "And Sherry Sterling, of course." I groaned.

"Sherry? I don't think so, Brit. Last I heard, she was going to be a teacher."

I felt my face turning bright red. Although I wanted to

keep my mouth shut I just couldn't. If Brian wasn't dating her, how in the heck did he know so much about her? I had to ask, "So how do you know so much about Sterling?" I was sure our fairy tale day was about to come to an end. Brian was still dating Sherry, or still liked her, anyway. She'd been to visit him at the Naval Academy, they went to prom together and Brian knew more about her than I knew about myself. So what was the deal?

Brian got quiet. "This is a hard thing to talk about."

I spoke, slightly annoyed, "I can handle it, if you're still dating her I just wish you would have told me before——"

He cut me off, "I'm not dating her, Brit. I've never dated her." He paused. "I don't know if you know this or not, but Sherry's mother passed away during her junior year of high school." Brian's face grew pale. "I got to know Sherry because my mom and her mom were best friends. That's why she and I went to prom together. I knew what a tough time she was having and wanted to be a good friend to her." His tone lightened, "It all worked out because that's when we met Josh, my roommate at the Academy. After prom, we went to a comedy club and he was there. We hit it off and Josh and I decided to put in a request to be roommates. And Josh and Sherry really hit it off. They've been dating ever since. That's why she came up to visit, she was seeing him."

I felt so stupid that I didn't know what to say. "I'm sorry, Brian."

He continued, "And when I said she was misunderstood–did you know she's got nine younger brothers and sisters that she looks after? Not an easy job. And that's why there *is no WNBA in her future. She can't leave her family. This Olympic team is going to be the end of her basketball career."*

Everything I didn't know about Sherry Sterling came rushing toward me in a tidal wave and suddenly I felt bad about the way I'd treated her. We'd both been chasing the same dream and although she'd done nothing wrong, her dream would soon end, while mine continued. I could talk to my mother on the phone whenever I felt like it, but Sherry couldn't. Life seemed pretty unfair for a moment. Tears welled up in my eyes. I had misunderstood Sherry. She wasn't mean, she was sad. She wasn't rude either, she was just weighed down by her responsibilities. And she wasn't a dirty player, she just had a lot more at stake. "Everything makes sense to me now, Brian. I owe Sherry an apology."

"Maybe you guys can become friends now and we can double-date." Brian said.

"So, you want to date me now?" I smiled sarcastically.

"Yeah," he said, leaning in to kiss me again.

In the first week of my junior season, Coach Hollins appointed me as the starting point guard. This meant that I'd beaten out Pip, a senior who played the position last year. This type of thing can be disruptive to a team, but while she was disappointed, Pip was a good sport about it. I was excited because Rosa and I were finally going to play in the same backcourt together.

Our biggest rivals all year were Virginia Central and my old pal Sherry Sterling, who was by now known exclusively as "Starling." We split the regular season games, each winning once at home. With a record of 19 and 7 we'd finished number one in our conference with Virginia Central right behind us at number two. Not surprisingly, the conference final found us matched up again. And it was a close game.

With just under six minutes remaining, we were knotted at 65. I brought the ball up and tossed it to Clarissa who nailed a three-pointer. The UNV students erupted in cheers. That's another good thing about winning——your classmates rally around you. After having nobody care about us during my first two years, by my junior season, we had scores of fans cheering us on.

Up by three with five minutes left, I became too concerned with Starling driving past me. I backpedaled to defend her, and the moment the ball touched her hands, she fired a three. I jumped, but wasn't close. Swish! Tie game.

I rushed the ball back up the floor, slinging it over to Jen, who tossed it to Leesha. She put it up from the paint and it bounced off the rim, but Clarissa tapped in the rebound. Back up by two. On the ensuing play, Starling put another shot up the moment she touched the ball. This time, I managed to nip it with my middle finger and knock it off-target. Clarissa leaped into the air and came down with the rebound.

We raced back toward our own goal. Seeing a lane, Clarissa drove hard to the basket. But just as she stepped into the paint, a body flew in from nowhere and accidentally tripped her up. She fell to the floor hard. We surrounded her instantly, as she hugged her knees to her chest, holding her right ankle and groaning. Our trainer came out and helped her sit up, then a couple of us assisted her off the court. Since Clarissa couldn't take her foul shots, Coach told me to. I popped them both in neatly, so distraught about Clarissa's leg that I could barely see the basket.

Central inbounded the ball with one minute left, down by four. We covered their two guard so closely she barely got the ball across the half-court line before being called for a ten-second violation. I grabbed for the ball, but she managed to flip it off to Starling. Swish! This time from inside the three-point line. We led by only two points now.

With fifty seconds left I passed the ball over to Ming. The pass was a little low and Ming never really got control of it. She was easily stripped and we gave chase down the court. I was in Starling's back pocket, and when she reached the three-point line, I jumped in front of her. She quickly passed the ball off to Karen Lutz, who chucked a long three-pointer that miraculously bounced off the backboard and in. (No way she meant to do that!) That quickly, we found ourselves down by two with just thirty seconds remaining.

I brought the ball up, dribbling patiently as the clock ticked down. I wanted to wait for one final shot to send the game into overtime. Rosa and I exchanged the ball a couple of times, trying to get someone open. Finally I set a pick for her and she drove to the lane. She was stopped by three converging defenders. "Clock!" I shouted as Rosa dribbled near the foul line with only nine seconds remaining. Immediately, she panicked and fired off a shot from the post. The ball rattled around the rim but didn't fall. Ming was right there to grab the board.

"Three seconds left!" Clarissa screamed from the bench. Quickly, Ming slung the ball out to me at the top of the key. I had no choice but to fire up a long three-pointer——not the shot that we'd planned for. All eyes were on the ball. It looked to be on line but I couldn't be sure. The buzzer sounded as the ball made a rainbow toward the basket.

A moment later I pumped my fist as the orange leather swished through the net. My first game-winning shot. Starling gave me a terrible look as she exited the court, but I just smiled at her. I couldn't have been more excited.

We were still standing on each other's shoulders celebrating when Rosa told me that Clarissa just left the stadium in an ambulance. An early medical report raised concerns about her Achilles tendon. That really put a damper on our celebration. An injury like that would end Clarissa's season.

The next day, our fears were realized. Clarissa had torn her Achilles. But hobbling on crutches, she came along with us to our first round game of the NCAA tournament. (We'd been invited for the second straight year.) Our first two games would be played out in Cleveland, Ohio. We had high hopes that we'd be successful even without our star player. But unfortunately, we were blown out by Tennessee College in the first round.

By the time classes started the fall of our senior year at UNV, Clarissa's Achilles tendon was completely healed. She'd rehabbed hard and we had a great feeling about the year ahead. We began our Sunday afternoon get-togethers as soon as fall semester got under way, not wanting to waste a second in getting everyone to think as a team.

Although I had hoped we would win a National Championship during my time at UNV, I was also pretty realistic about it.

After all, the school had never made it past the second round. But this year felt different somehow. We were a team in every sense of the word and when we stepped onto the court we almost always excelled.

Personally, I had a great season, averaging over fourteen points a game and nearly ten assists. As a team, we lost only four games, winning twenty-one. So when we entered the conference tournament this year, we were the favorite to win the thing! Although Southern Maryland gave us a run for our money in the conference tournament, eventually the final game pitted us against Sherry Sterling and Virginia Central.

This year, however, we had little trouble putting old Starling away. We were devastating on the inside and cruised to our second straight conference championship, marking the first time in school history that UNV had won that title two years in a row.

A few weeks later, the NCAA tournament began. Things couldn't have gone any better early on. We'd gotten the invite for a third straight year, setting another school record. And somehow, we cruised to victory in both of our first two games, making it to the sweet sixteen for the first time in school history. The sweet sixteen was the round in the tournament where only sixteen teams remained from the original sixty-four. No other UNV basketball team (men's or women's) had ever made it to the sweet sixteen. Getting there put us two wins away from the final four.

When we got on a flight to New Orleans for our sweet sixteen matchup, I don't think I could have been more excited. We spent the first day just taking in our surroundings, as our game wasn't until the following night. The spring breeze was warm and gentle as we walked toward the French Quarter. Jazz spilled out onto the streets and Clarissa stopped now and then to tap dance with the little boys performing on the corners. Andrea and Jen tried on one Mardi Gras mask after another and we all lined up to take a streetcar ride. Meanwhile, I spent a long time outside of an art gallery looking at a painting of a tiny blue dog lost among a crowd of big brown dogs. I know it sounds crazy, but the blue dog reminded me of myself. I was always the blue dog on the basketball court.

But when Saturday evening came, I couldn't think about dogs or paintings or anything for that matter. All that mattered was the game. Once again, we were happy to be here. After all, we were the lowest-ranked team in the field of sixteen. The media had labeled us the "Cinderella" team, which meant that we were overachievers and that other teams took us lightly because we weren't usually a squad to be reckoned with. Still, it was like a dream come true. I couldn't believe how far I'd come since that first time back at Jefferson when I didn't even make the JV team.

Unfortunately, we drew Northern California State, the number one team in the nation. We managed to stay with them early and actually led by one point at halftime. But by the end of the third quarter, we found ourselves trailing by eight, and three of our starters were playing with four fouls each. It was fun while it lasted, and then things got a little ugly. By midway through the fourth quarter, they started to wear us down and stretched their lead to twenty.

I'd love to tell you that we came back and triumphed, but

that isn't what happened. Although we made a decent run in the second half, we came up short and lost by twelve to an excellent team. For Clarissa though, the game was a coming-out party. On one of the last plays of the game, I collected a loose ball and threw a pass to her at the other end of the court. She caught the ball and leaped toward the rim, slamming home a dunk on national television, in front of thousands of viewers. The entire place went crazy and it was all anyone could talk about after the game. Because we're not as tall and can't jump as high, girls usually don't dunk. But when we do, everyone gets excited. I think her dunk made more headlines that night on SportsCenter than any other game in the tournament. Needless to say, it was great exposure for her in terms of getting drafted by a WNBA team.

Sure, there were some tears in the locker room after the game. Today was the last game for Clarissa, Ming, Andrea, and I. We'd grown very close in the years we'd played at UNV and now we'd have to move on. It was a bittersweet time in our lives, a rite of passage. So we cried for all the good times and the great friends we'd made. Overall, I think we were satisfied. We'd accomplished more than I ever could have dreamed of as a freshman at UNV. Two conference titles and a senior season that would go down as the greatest in UNV history! We'd put Northern Virginia on the basketball map. Now everyone had heard of our little school. So when we flew back home the next day, our heads were held high.

CHAPTER ELEVEN

A LONG STRANGE DAY

Brian heaved a deep sigh of frustration. "I should have taken you back to the airport. I was just having so much fun and I wanted you to love San Francisco. I should have——"

I cut him off. "I'm a big girl, Brian. I did what I wanted to do." I was angry with myself. I could see my Olympic dream slipping through my fingers all because of my lack of self-discipline. I looked at the clock—5:03. I had twenty-seven minutes before the plane started boarding.

"Well, nobody could have anticipated an earthquake, right? I'm sure the coach will understand." Brian was trying to talk me into thinking that everything would work out.

I wasn't buying it. "She wouldn't understand if the ground opened up and swallowed me whole, Brian," I muttered grimly.

The traffic began to move. "At least then you wouldn't

have to worry about being late." He smiled and looked out into the distance. "So tell me, did anybody steal your heart at UNV when I wasn't looking?"

"Some have tried," I spoke flippantly, "but none have succeeded." What I didn't tell him was that he was the standard by which I'd measured every guy I'd ever met. Not that I didn't have a great time in college, and not that I didn't make some close friends. It's just that I never fell in love with anybody else because I'd always been in love with Brian.

He laughed and seemed to like my attempt at a joke. I flipped on the radio and we held hands, listening to music quietly for the next few minutes. We'd talked for about two hours straight, and as we sat in silence I thought about how nice it was just to be there with him. So nice, in fact, that I almost forgot about the time. Almost. When I did glance down at the dash, the numbers on the clock seemed to get bigger and bigger. I just couldn't tear my eyes away. "Five-ten Brian. We're not going to make it, are we?" Reality was starting to set in.

"Sure we are," he responded. And suddenly the car was swerving out of the line of traffic and turning into a gas station.

"Don't tell me we're out of gas, too." I moaned, the bad luck really getting to me now. Brian didn't answer. He just jumped out of the car and raced over to the station attendant, who was standing in the garage. I watched them speak for a few seconds and then hopped out of the car to see what had gone wrong this time. Brian shook the man's greasy hand and flipped him the keys to the car. I walked a few steps closer to them.

"Helmets?" I heard Brian ask.

"What?" I began.

The man handed us two helmets. I put mine on, completely confused. Then the guy handed us a set of keys. Brian took me by the hand and led me over to a bright blue motorcycle. "Hop on, Brit," he grinned.

Now normally I wouldn't just hop on a motorcycle and start riding into the sunset, but this was different. I had to get to the airport. As I hopped onto the motorcycle I caught a glance at the words written on the side. Call it coincidence, call it fate, but the motorcycle we were riding was called Blue Dog. Right as I read those words I started laughing. Maybe everything would work out.

I hugged Brian tight as he started the engine. He waved to the attendant and yelled over the noisy bike, "I should be back in about an hour. Thank you so much."

"Thank you," I waved goodbye and held on tight for my first motorcycle ride. Brian maneuvered the big machine along the edge of the roadway and we began to pick up speed. "I think we've got a clear shot to the airport, now," Brian shouted over his shoulder as I tightened my arms around him. We roared away alongside the piled-up cars. My heart was racing almost as fast as the motorcycle as we zipped in between and around the miles of traffic backed up as far as the eye could see. The wind and fog poured in from the ocean and I hugged Brian tighter. In only a short while, we were on the freeway.

"Not long now," Brian called over his shoulder. The traffic was still heavy but it was moving fairly well.

As we eased off onto the airport exit, I stole a look at my watch, 5:44. The plane was probably getting ready to take-off. Brian pulled the motorcycle up to the curb and jumped off. "Let's go, Brit!" He grabbed my hand and we raced to the ticket counter, which was swamped with huge lines of passengers. I could feel the tears pooling in the corners of my eyes. The terminal clock read 5:49. Then I saw Brian behind the counter, gesturing wildly at one of the customer service reps, even as he was motioning for me to join him.

"Your ticket, Brit, give him your ticket!" Brian commanded.

I managed to fish the ticket out of my purse, my famously quick hands suddenly all thumbs. "OK," Brian gushed, pumping the man's hand as he handed me back a stamped ticket. An instant later Brian was pulling me toward the security check. "You got everything, Brit?"

I just looked at him dumbly. Everything was happening too fast. Finally, I forced out the words. "My gym bag."

He stopped short. "Where is it?"

"The lockers," I answered.

He looked around quickly and spun me off in the direction of the lockers. "Key!" he shouted and I handed it to him. He shoved the key in, but it wouldn't work. "Try again," I yelled.

He did, but it wouldn't open. "Give me a quarter," he shouted.

"What?" I asked.

"A quarter. If I put another quarter in, it'll open." I searched my pockets and couldn't find one. The clock now read 5:54. Finally, I knew what I had to do. I pulled off my sneaker

and grabbed my lucky Washington state quarter, handing it to Brian. He looked at it for a second before sliding it into the slot, "You're still lucky, Brit, don't worry."

And to be honest, I wasn't. Giving up the quarter that had brought me luck for so long wasn't that big of a deal to me. After this whole Sherry Sterling thing I realized that luck wasn't something controlled by quarters. Life wasn't quite that simple. All the lucky quarters in the world wouldn't have cured Mrs. Sterling's cancer.

In an instant the quarter was a distant memory. Brian jerked out my bag, shoved it into my hands, and propelled me toward the security check again. He made some sort of excuse to the other passengers in the line and they let us cut in front. The guard made an exception and let Brian go through the checkpoint with me. (That uniform worked wonders for him.) We raced down the corridor together.

"Last gate," he panted, "wouldn't you know it?"

I grinned, finally realizing I was going to make it to Los Angeles after all. When we reached the end of the tunnel, Brian explained my plight to the airline attendant who was about to close the jet-way door.

"Quickly!" the attendant prodded.

Brian pulled me aside before I boarded the plane and kissed me. It was the greatest kiss of my life, far surpassing the kiss on the observation deck.

"I've missed you, Brian." I whispered against his hair.

Brian smiled his glorious smile. He kissed my hand and let it go. I raced toward the plane. Just before I disappeared, I heard him shout. "I'll call you every day, Brittany!"

"Seat 11-A," the young man at the aircraft door said, and I hurried in, tossing my gym bag overhead and collapsing into the seat to fasten my belt as the plane began to pull away from the gate. When I melted into the comfort of that cushion my head was absolutely spinning. My entire life had just been turned upside down. Did I have a boyfriend? Was it Brian? I took a deep breath, forgetting everything. I turned my head to my right and glanced at the passenger in the seat next to me.

In a final twist of fate, I found myself staring into the pretty eyes of Sherry Sterling. As we flew over the tall California mountains, we chatted like old friends. Our rivalry was forgotten as we journeyed together to the next stage. I apologized for the way I acted over the years and she did the same. I told her about Brian and she mentioned that she and Josh had just gotten engaged. Then we both got giddy talking about what it would be like to compete in the Olympics.

I stepped off the plane in Los Angeles and everything had changed. I had Brian, Sherry Sterling and I were friends, and I had spent a wonderful day in San Francisco. My life had a clear focus. I was a little blue dog with a great big heart. Was I going to make the Olympic team? Maybe, maybe not. As usual, I was a long shot.

TEST YOURSELF... ARE YOU A PROFESSIONAL READER?

Chapter 1: The List

Name a few reasons why Brittany enjoyed playing point guard.

Explain the differences between Brittany and Clarissa on the basketball court.

How did Brittany stumble upon her love of photography?

ESSAY

In this chapter Brittany tells us that she enjoys the opportunity to be the point guard, the leader on the basketball court. Detail a time in your life when you stepped forward to be a leader. How did that make you feel? Did you learn anything about yourself from this experience?

Chapter 2: A Natural

Who is Susan Ambler? Why doesn't Brittany like her?

How was Brittany's concentration broken during tryouts?

Why did the strongest aspect of Brittany's basketball game abandon her during tryouts? Name that aspect.

ESSAY

In Chapter 2, Brittany is stunned when she fails to make the girls junior varsity basketball team. Detail a disappointment in your life. How did you get over that disappointment? What positives did you take from this experience?

Chapter 3: Layover

What had Brittany done to prepare herself for her second year of junior varsity basketball tryouts?

Why did Brittany pay close attention to the games when she was on the bench?

What did Brian give Brittany before the final cuts for the junior varsity team? Why?

ESSAY

Brittany's actions in this chapter define the word "perseverance." Detail a time in your life when you persevered and overcame odds on your way to success.

Chapter 4: Losing It

What conclusions did Brittany come to after watching her "team" from the bench during the first half of her sophomore year?

Why did Brittany get the opportunity to start the game against Shenendoah?

What thought cheered Brittany up after the game against Shenendoah in which she received a technical foul?

ESSAY

In this chapter, Brittany loses her temper and Coach Holt benches her as a result. Due to her tirade, Brittany doesn't see much more playing time during that season. She eventually realizes that losing her temper didn't help the situation. Detail a time in your life when you lost your temper. Why did you regret the outburst? What did you learn from this incident that helped you in the future?

Chapter 5: Coach Jensen

When Brian and Brittany discuss their high school years, what realization do they make about why they never dated?

What reasoning did Coach Jensen offer to Brittany as to why she would be better suited for another year of junior varsity?

What routine does Brittany's father follow when he is faced with a difficult decision?

ESSAY

In Chapter 5, Brittany dedicates herself and her time to becoming a better basketball player. She reads about the game and practices whenever she can. Detail how reading, knowledge, and hard work will help you as you chase your dream.

Chapter 6: Things Get Ugly

What changes did Brittany help induce in the overall play of Sandi Powers?

Why did Brittany have to wear a "visual appliance" after the game versus Madison?

Why did Brittany receive such anger from her teammates before the big game?

ESSAY

In this chapter, we are given proof that cruel words do hurt. Brittany suffers greatly because of the criticism of her teammates. Describe how Brittany is affected by her teammates' negative comments. What did these words do to her self-confidence?

Chapter 7: Sherry Sterling

Who is Marc Iaccone?

According to Brittany, what aspects of her game set her apart from other talented players across the country?

Despite the reality that no colleges were making a fuss over Brittany Bristol, what recognition off the court marked Brittany as a success?

ESSAY

Throughout this book we learn that Brittany is not a quitter, that she has a strong work ethic and a heart for the game. As you chase your dream, what are some qualities that you have that will enable you to accomplish great things in life?

Chapter 8: Northern Virginia

Why did the "chemistry" in Northern Virginia's locker room begin to further deteriorate when Clarissa Jackson arrived?

What did Clarissa do to try and bridge the gap between her and the rest of the Northern Virginia team?

Why were Brittany and the rest of the freshman class very much looking forward to their sophomore season?

ESSAY

In this chapter, we read about how many of the upperclassmen went out of their way to make newcomer, Clarissa Jackson, feel uncomfortable. They acted this way without even taking the time to get to know her. Name a time in your life when you were guilty of judging someone before you actually took the time to know them.

What did this teach you?

Chapter 9: Sophomore Year

Why did Brittany enjoy her job working as a counselor at a basketball camp during the summer before her sophomore year?

Despite not being in the starting lineup, why did Brittany consider her sophomore season a success?

Why did UNV's excitement wane when they walked onto the floor for their game against Southern Maryland?

ESSAY

Something as simple as Sunday evening cookie parties obviously helps UNV's team chemistry and camaraderie. The girls grow to become friends outside of the basketball court. Why would this friendship and closeness help a team play better basketball? Detail some differences between the UNV team during Brittany's freshman and sophomore seasons.

Chapter 10: Inch by Inch

How had Brittany misunderstood Sherry Sterling? What didn't Brittany know about Sherry's personal life?

What situation put a damper on UNV's victory over Virginia Central?

How did UNV fare in the NCAA tournament during Brittany's junior season?

In this chapter we are aware of the bittersweet time in Brittany's life, and in all the lives of her senior teammates as they prepare to leave college. Brittany and her teammates are torn between moving on with their lives and remembering all the great times they had in college. Detail a time in your life when "moving on" was bittersweet. How did this experience make you feel?

Chapter 11: A Long, Strange Day

Why did Brittany laugh when she hopped onto the motorcycle with the words "'Blue Dog'" written on the side?

Why did Brittany have to give up her lucky quarter?

What in Brittany's life had changed when she stepped off the plane in Los Angeles?

Congratulations! You have completed another Scobre book. What did you learn from Brittany's life and the way in which she chased her dreams? How do you plan on making your dreams come true?